A JURY OF
ONE'S FEARS

ANNETTE LACKNER

A Jury of One's Fears

ISBN: 978-1-7359194-5-4

For information, contact the author:

Annette Lackner
6561 Devonwood Dr.
Cincinnati, Ohio 45224

Email: tonibell@fuse.net
Website: annettelackner.com

Published by:

Chilidog Press LLC
pbronson@chilidogpress.com

Chilidog Press
Loveland, Ohio
www.chilidogpress.com

Cover photos:
gavel: Valery Evlakhov/Shutterstock.com
cabin: iStock.com/Lana2011

Cover and interior design by: Craig Ramsdell, Ramsdell Design

Dedication

This book is dedicated to the many
strong women who have influenced my life.

CONTENTS

1
JULIA

She could see the setting sun in the rearview mirror as the music blared on her favorite station. He'd never let her play the radio when they were traveling together. She realized she'd be able to play music whenever she liked now. The thought of that filled her with sheer joy. She'd be able to do all sorts of things in her new home, things she never could have imagined a few years ago. She'd be able to go out with friends after a nursing shift without facing his anger when she came home. She'd be able to see Krista whenever she liked, and not listen to grumbling about how it inconvenienced his schedule when she visited their daughter at Georgetown.

The sun's orange-colored aura surrounded her and with it came the realization that it would be dark soon. Her goal was to reach the Maryland Welcome Center before sunset. Her sister's "Goodbye" echoed in her ears. "Be careful traveling alone."

Julia had laughed and told her sister she would be doing all sorts of things by herself now. The one thing she would not do was drink. That was in the past, along with all the other ugly parts of her life.

Julia focused straight ahead. Her horrible marriage and alcoholism were behind her and now a good nursing career in Maryland awaited her, not far from Krista and Georgetown. This was one big adventure. An adventure the abused, cowering, mousey little woman she was a few years ago could never have imagined in her wildest dreams.

She glanced down at the empty, Jumbo Size cup in her console, another splurge on her part. He hated her drinking soda because he felt that healthy, fit people only drank bottled water or juices. It was all about appearances for him. She bought the biggest one listed on the drive-thru menu just because now she could. A stop would be necessary. When she saw the sign "Rest Area Next Exit," she gave a sigh of relief. She entered the access ramp and crept up the hill past the truck area, then eased into a space in the section for cars. She started to grab the empty burger box on the passenger seat, another no-no in the eyes of her ex, but decided to get it on her way back, fearing she wouldn't get to the restroom in time. Clicking the "lock" button on her key fob she realized there were no other people or cars around. A black SUV pulled up a couple of spots away. She recalled seeing one just like it at her last Rest Area stop, and somehow that memory brought a shiver up her spine. "Oh, stop it," she told herself, "You're not that whiney little thing anymore."

The facility was a typical rest stop building except for the garden of Black-Eyed Susans flanking the cement walkway. She sailed through the glass doors. The emptiness of the space echoed the eerie sound of her lonely footsteps.

She dashed into the stall. Oh, at last relief! The door on the stall next to hers opened then closed. She zipped up her jeans and reached for her purse dangling from the chrome hook on the back of the door. She froze. The feet in the stall next to hers! They had on men's work shoes. She took a deep breath to calm herself as all sorts of horrible thoughts began to fill her head. Julia rationalized that lots of women wear men's work shoes; she probably works here. Just to be safe, I'll just hurry out of here without washing my hands.

As she rushed for the door, she caught a glimpse of a huge, dark figure in the mirror. Terror seized her as she plunged for the door, but there was something around her neck pulling her back in. She was fighting to breathe, kicking and flailing. As the cord tightened, she saw her daughter's face just before the darkness engulfed her.

* * * * *

He knew the coast was clear. The man in black pulled her out of the restroom, holding her up as best he could. Using her keys, he opened her car and pushed her into the passenger side. He reached into his pocket, pulled out a flask and doused her with bourbon then threw the empty flask on the floor. The attacker got in on the driver's side and drove by the truck area, taking one last look at the woman before he eased onto the sloping exit ramp and waited for the right moment when an oncoming tractor-trailer would be unable to stop. Hand on the door handle, he stepped on the accelerator and jumped from the car.

He had to catch his breath as he crept back to the SUV and plopped his large frame in the driver's seat. The sound of screeching brakes and metal hitting metal still rang in his ears. A moment later he could see the flames illuminating the exit ramp.

Man, this one was hot. I would've liked a piece of that ass before I iced her. What a shame.

He sat back and smiled as he listened to the wailing sirens on the highway below. "What a cinch," he said out loud.

ANNETTE LACKNER

2
THE CABIN

The narrow gravel trail that led to the cabin was thick with foliage. Inside, flames from the fireplace cast shadows on the ten male visitors who came from all walks of life. In fact, outside of this woodland resort, their paths would not likely cross.

Their host led them to the well-stocked bar and offered them a drink. There wasn't much conversation. These men had nothing in common except their misleading hunting attire and the purpose of this meeting.

The distinguished looking facilitator, although dressed in hunting clothes, looked more like a model for the cover of an *Outdoor Life* magazine. His body was well toned, nails manicured and short beard well groomed. He gathered the men around the fireplace, pulled out a brief agenda and circulated it, giving instructions to throw it into the fire when the meeting ended.

The group went over their purpose and commitment and other old business. The leader then turned to a burly man.

"We have a report from Max. Max?"

The man to whom he directed the question stood up and looked at his agenda. "Item number one has been taken care of. All neat and tidy, no blowback." Max searched the face of the man who introduced him for some kind of reaction, but detected nothing. *"God he is one cold son of a bitch,"* Max thought.

"Good," then we can move to the next item on our list. What's the status, Max?"

"Plans are in the works. It should be a week or two before it's accomplished. I have a choice of methods. I just have to wait for the prime opportunity."

His boss smiled broadly, although his eyes remained dark and cold. "Great! Are we all still committed to the project?"

The group nodded in agreement.

"Please cross off item number one and move on to item number two."

The fellow "hunters" glanced at each other somberly and looked down at their papers. Item #2 simply said Maura. They crossed off Item #1 – **J U L I A**.

3
GWEN

She pushed through the revolving door into the Arnold Building. As Gwen waited for the elevator to take her up to Bailey's Detective Agency on the fifth floor, she glanced at the Far Horizons Travel Agency located directly across from her. Oh, how she would love to hop on a plane to some exotic destination. But there was one issue: lack of money.

The bell chimed, brass doors opened, and she floated into the elevator car thinking of drifting on a cruise somewhere. Gwen had only been on this job for six months. What she thought would be so exciting turned out to be extremely boring. Endless hours sitting outside of buildings in her car, watching people come and go, writing it all down, sometimes taking pictures with her phone. She wasn't sure how long she was going to last here, but she needed the income. A job at a friend's catering business when she needed extra help supplemented her income, but between the two she could just barely make ends meet.

Zeke Bailey was where he always was in the morning; sitting with his feet propped up on the desk, newspaper hiding his face, a cloud of smoke rising from behind.

"Hi boss," Gwen greeted him as she dropped her tote bag on the floor next to her workspace. "What's new in the world?"

His eyes peered over the paper. "Same old, same old. Everything in this city needs fixing, but nobody wants to pay for the fixing." He twisted around in the chair and put his feet on the floor. He looked up at Gwen. "You look great today, Babe." He took her in from her short blond hair, generous breasts and black pants to her slip-on plastic heels. He stood up and stretched his back.

Gwen bristled. She knew she was attractive to men. It was her curse. She tried to downplay her good looks by having her beautiful waves cut into a short style and by dressing in a way that didn't draw notice. She no longer wanted the attention of the male sex. It had brought her nothing but pain.

"Down boy," she teased. "Your wolf fangs are showing." She tried to keep it light because she really needed this job.

"I know, I know, I'm a happily married man, but I still appreciate an attractive woman when I see one. Sorry if I offended you."

She looked him in the eyes and smirked. "What's on the agenda today?"

He slipped on his suitcoat. "I have to go down to city hall to dig into some records. I don't have too much for you. Just handle the phones and finish organizing the files so that they make some kind of sense. As if anything in this world makes sense! I should be back around one or two. I'll keep in touch." He was out the door.

As soon as Zeke was gone, she opened the window to get rid of the smell of smoke. She poured herself a cup of cloudy coffee, snatched up the rumpled *Cincinnati Enquirer* and sat at his desk. She was glad her boss was a creature of habit and still bought the morning paper. She had her second husband to thank for her love of reading the newspaper. He wanted her to be informed when they were out to dinner with his friends, as long she didn't voice disagreement with his opinions. That was one mistake she didn't make a second time. She glanced at the headlines on the first page. Most of it she already learned from the morning news programs as she was getting dressed for the office. The more interesting news was usually on page two or three; the little buried items that usually turned into bigger stories in the not-too-distant future.

Gwen's heart skipped a beat when she caught sight of an article on the obituary page.

"Ex-wife of local judge, David Kildeer, killed in car accident, alcohol suspected."

The accompanying picture showed a lovely, dark-haired woman in a nurse's uniform. Gwen read on.

Julia Kildeer was killed last week on Interstate 68. Relatives say she was on her way to a nursing position in Montgomery County, Maryland. Police reports said her auto sped off an exit ramp onto I-68, causing a nine-car pileup. Eight additional drivers were injured, none fatally. The accident report said alcohol was involved. Judge Kildeer had no comment, except to ask for privacy for his grief-stricken family.

Gwen leaned over the desk, resting her chin in her hands as she stared at the picture above the article. She couldn't believe it. This was her casual friend Julia from the Women Recovering from Abuse support group. Although they never knew last names, the picture was definitely "her" Julia. They always talked during the coffee break. Beautiful Julia dead! She recalled the abuse Julia had described. Everything from being locked in her room for days, to bruises and broken ribs. And to think her husband was the reputable Judge David Kildeer! It reinforced her opinion that all men were sons of bitches. Judge Kildeer's picture was always in the papers, attending fundraisers, commenting on criminal cases. What a joke!

She worked on the filing, trying to get Julia's picture out of her mind. She wondered what on earth made her friend start drinking again with so much to look forward to. It just didn't add up. She thought of her last conversation with Julia. It was her last meeting before she left town. She had beamed with the excitement of her new beginning in Maryland.

Zeke meandered back about 1 p.m. She showed him the paper and held back tears. She didn't want to give her boss any reason to put his hands on her. "I knew her from my support group. It just doesn't add up. She went through rehab. She had so much to live for."

He put his hand on her shoulder. "It happens all the time, Babe. Alcoholism is a nasty business. I've been there. Maybe the pressure of starting a new job just got to her. You know what they say: once an alcoholic, always an alcoholic. Why don't you go have a nice lunch? Take as long as you like. It's on me. I'll hold down the fort."

"I think I'll take you up on that. I'm really shook up. Thanks, Boss." She grabbed her tote and left the office in his care, knowing he would probably take a little nap.

When Gwen got off the elevator, she wandered over to the travel agency's window display. A beautiful South Seas island called to her. Repressed tears were clouding her vision as she pushed the door open right into a man who was exiting. Her tote and its abundance of necessary "junk" flew across the floor.

"Oh, I am so sorry!" she blurted out as the tears that had welled up escaped down her cheeks.

"No, no, it was all my fault." A nice-looking middle-aged guy began picking up the contents of her bag. "I wasn't paying attention to where I was going."

Blue eyes peered at her through horn-rimmed glasses. "Come sit down at my desk. You're obviously upset." He guided her to a cubicle, sat her down and handed her a box of tissues. Gwen blew her nose while he retrieved the rest of her belongings.

"Here we go." He placed the canvas tote on his desk. "I hope I didn't upset you to tears." He smiled at her. "Your bag can't be that valuable," he teased.

She looked up and smiled. He was very good looking. A bit of a nerd, but still good looking. He reminded her of Harrison Ford as the young Indiana Jones.

"It was my fault. I just found out an acquaintance was killed in an accident. My mind wasn't where it should be." Gwen made an effort to compose herself. "Do you work here?"

"I'm the owner, which isn't as glamorous as it sounds; lots of time staring at a computer screen. Look, I was just going to lunch. Can I at least take you along to make up for running you over? I have a good shoulder, if you need to talk about your friend. I was going to try the new Thai restaurant down the street. Are you on your lunch hour? I've seen you taking the elevator in the morning. I presume you work in the building." He stammered a little.

Gwen continued to wipe her eyes with the damp tissue. She found it endearing that he seemed a little nervous about asking her to join him for lunch.

"I'd like that. I really don't want to eat alone today."

He held out a well-manicured hand. "I'm Jack Manley."

She put her hand in his. "Gwen Hubbard."

The Thai restaurant was a block away, situated amid several new restaurants that had recently opened in the trendy old neighborhood. He gently placed his hand on her elbow as they crossed the street. Gwen immediately moved it away once they were back on the sidewalk.

They were seated in a booth in a back corner. "Do you like hot or mild?" he asked.

She took a good look at him as he perused the menu. He was very handsome in a straightlaced kind of way. Not the type she usually fell for. But then she was married twice to total losers. She hadn't fared well with the he-man type. Gwen sensed she wasn't in the same class with this guy and reminded herself that all men were sons of bitches.

"I'll just have the soup and the salad featured with the lunch specials. Just tell them zero heat."

He looked at her and smiled as the waitress poured their water. "Where do you work in the building?"

"Bailey's Detective Agency, fifth floor."

"I know Zeke from my previous life. I had a law practice. Zeke did some work for us. I get a kick out of the film noir image he likes to portray. Well, this is a first. I've never had lunch with a female detective before." He ran his hand through his sandy hair.

"Oh, I'm not a detective, just the peon who does the grunt work."

He continued to ask her about what she did.

"It's mostly tailing cheating husbands and wives. Keeping track of where they go and how long they are there, that type of thing."

"Speaking of spouses, are you married?"

Gwen couldn't believe it, but he actually blushed when he asked the question.

"Twice. Both were losers and abusers. I just seem to fall for the wrong guys."

His blue eyes rested on her. "I'm so sorry."

"Well, so am I. What about you?" She placed the colorful silk napkin on her lap.

"I was. My wife died of cancer four years ago. We owned a law practice together. I was sort of lost without her. I decided to get out of the legal field and try something different.

We were always going to travel, but never found the time. That's how I ended up in the industry."

"Well, I have lots of time, but not the money. I was really screwed financially by both my ex-husbands. It's too long of a story to go into over lunch."

The waitress arrived with their food as he asked about what had happened to her friend.

Gwen began to nibble on her salad. She had to be careful about what she said since her support group meetings were confidential and the members were anonymous. "I just saw it in the paper. She was killed in a car accident in Maryland. Julia and I both attended the same group. She had come such a long way since I first met her. She was on her way to a new job in Maryland. It just doesn't make sense to me. She was a recovering alcoholic and had so much to live for. They said alcohol was involved. I just saw her two weeks ago and she seemed so happy and eager to start her new career. It just doesn't add up."

"A lot of things in life just don't make sense. I guess we're better off just accepting them and going forward," Jack said. "I'm speaking from experience." Gwen noticed a cloud of sorrow creep over his face.

"Do you ever go to any of those exotic places you advertise at your agency?" she asked, trying to change the subject before she started crying again.

He peered over his glasses. "Oh sure, but it's not that much fun when you don't have someone you can share it with." Another blush. "I like Hawaii, but what's not to like about Hawaii? My favorite so far is the Galapagos Islands. Lots of wildlife, very pristine and exotic, like nothing you've ever seen. You should come by and I'll show you the brochures."

He looked down at his beeping phone. "Oh darn, I have to be back for a meeting soon, but you stay as long as you like." He picked up the bill. "It's on me, with apologies."

She smiled. "I'll stay a little longer. I need to get my emotions in check before I go back to the office."

She watched him pay the bill, then stop and wave from the bamboo-curtained door. "Don't forget to stop in, I'll show you the Galapagos," he called.

Gwen's eyes followed him as he hurried down the street. He was really a good-looking man... if you were looking for one. She reminded herself that she was through with men. They all seem nice at first, until you marry them. But then, she thought, nothing says you have to get married. One can keep one's freedom.

Gwen drank the last sip of tea in her cup, then picked up her bag, deciding she should probably go to her "Abuse Meeting" this evening on her way home from work. Maybe there would be more news about Julia.

* * * * *

The usual people were standing outside of the high school gym, smoking one last cigarette before they entered. Gwen crossed the parking lot and said "Hi." Some she knew, some she didn't. However, she did know their stories of the abuse that brought them to this place.

She opened the swinging door and descended the steps to the gym. Jen, the leader, was setting up folding chairs in a circle. Gwen laid down her purse and started to help. Jen pushed back a wisp of hair from her brow and tucked it behind her ear. "Thanks, Gwen."

"I guess you heard about Julia?" Gwen whispered.

"Yeah, I am going to mention her at the beginning of our session in case some of them recognized her picture in the paper."

"It just doesn't make sense to me. She seemed to be in such a good place." Gwen filled in the last space with a chair.

"Can you stay after and chat?" Jen asked.

Gwen's interest was piqued at this unusual request from Jen. The facilitator usually kept a safe professional distance from her members. "Sure," she replied as they sat down and the women outside came in to take their places.

The meeting was the usual two hours filled with stories of where these women were in their healing processes. Getting one last cup of coffee during the break, Gwen turned to a woman who was wiping her eyes, saying, "I just can't believe it! She was so excited about her future in Maryland."

"I know," another woman chimed in. "I can't believe it either, beautiful Julia dead."

She had so much to live for. I was so shocked when I saw her picture in the paper this morning!"

"After all that she overcame, to die in an accident. It just seems so unfair," a heavy-set woman commented.

When the meeting room finally emptied, Jen sat down and patted a chair for Gwen to join her. Gwen accepted the offer and took a seat.

Jen said, "I just wanted to tell you that Julia's sister contacted me today. Julia was visiting her in West Virginia right before the accident. She said there was no way Julia was drinking that night. Her sister said she was upbeat and excited about starting her new life in Maryland."

"Did she say anything to the police about it?"

"Yes, but she didn't get anywhere. I probably shouldn't tell you this, but…."

"Yes?" Gwen took a deep breath more certain that something wasn't right.

"She thinks Julia's husband had something to do with it. We know what an abuser he was. But he is a very powerful man, and anything said here is confidential. We wouldn't even know who he was if her picture hadn't been in the paper."

Gwen recalled some of Julia's stories. "He did some pretty awful things to her. Do you think it could have been revenge for taking him to court or something like that?"

"It could be. Now that we know who he is, I don't remember seeing anything in the papers about a scandal, or their divorce. He always comes across as a pillar of virtue. But then we know from these meetings that appearances can be deceiving."

They folded up the remaining chairs and stacked them against the wall.

"Well, like you said, he's a very powerful man," Gwen said. "I'm going to check some things out. Maybe my boss can help. I work for a private detective."

Jen placed her hand on Gwen's arm. "Please, keep me posted. I just have an uneasy feeling about the whole thing."

"If I find anything out, I'll let you know."

They walked to the empty parking lot and got into their cars.

"Good night." Jen waved as she drove away.

Gwen dreaded going back to her dismal apartment. Its main asset was that the rent was cheap. She had been furnishing it from second-hand stores and antique shops for the last six months. She had picked up area rugs on-line to add more interest and color to the solid-colored furnishings. Although it wasn't the professionally decorated home that she had lived in during her second marriage, it was beginning to feel like home. The first thing she did when she got inside the door was kick off her heels, and stretch. She felt her cat Ethel rub against her calf. "You won't let me feel lonely tonight, will you?" She picked up the calico cat and held it close to her face. "Let's feed you." Gwen had noticed Ethel hanging around outside her apartment for days and finally took her in. She posted a note in the rental office, but no one claimed the stray cat. Gwen decided she could use the company and took her in permanently. She always considered herself more of a dog person, but now she could see the advantages of a cat. All you need is a litter box and food. She was surprised by how much the cat took to her, and how much she was beginning to care for the cat.

She emptied a tin of cat food into a bowl and placed it on the floor, then poured herself a glass of Merlot and curled up on the sofa. She had to unwind before going to bed. The meetings always dredged up the awful memories of abuse she had suffered. Two marriages: two abusers. She was working on figuring out why she was drawn to that kind of man.

She began to doze.

* * * * *

Gwen was under the bed with her little sister. "Shhhhh." Ali continued to cry. "But he's hurting Mommy," she sniveled. They could hear
Mommy screaming as he threw her around. They could hear his blows.
"Just be quiet or it will get worse." She wrapped herself around Ali,
trying to comfort her. They were trembling with fear and then with one
big swoop the bedspread was gone. Daddy's crazed eyes were staring
in. "NO!" she screamed. "NO!" She jumped up off the couch, spilling
the wine. Ethel leapt off the chair and ran to her side.

   "It's okay, kitty, it was just a bad dream."

ANNETTE LACKNER

4
TWO LUNCHES

"Hello," someone called as Gwen waited for the elevator. She turned and there was the young Harrison Ford advancing toward her.

"I just wanted to apologize for cutting lunch so short. Can I make up for it today?"

"Oh," she said, trying not to be dazzled by his great smile. She hesitated a second and then caved. "Why not? You can tell me about some more of those exotic places." She looked at her watch. "Is one o'clock okay?"

"You got it. Meet down here at the agency?"

"Sure."

When she got to the office, Zeke was in his usual position behind the newspaper.

He looked up and gave her the daily once over. "You feeling better today?"

She sat down in her swivel chair and began to gently twist back and forth. "Julia's sister contacted our group facilitator. She felt it didn't add up either. She thinks Julia's husband was involved, but she didn't get anywhere with the police."

"Well, there's not much you can do. Just remember, people always look for someone to blame when something like this happens. Let it rest a while and you'll feel better about the whole thing."

Gwen pushed the gold bracelet up her arm, not feeling consoled by Zeke's advice. "Do you mind if I take lunch at one? Will you be here?"

Zeke raised his eyebrows. "Sure. You got a date?"

"Well, sort of. The guy who owns the travel agency in the lobby asked me to lunch. I ran into him yesterday, literally. He seems like a pretty nice guy."

Zeke put the paper down on top of a pile of manila folders. "Oh, you mean Jack Manley. He is a nice guy. I worked with him a little when he had a law practice with his wife. She was a great gal . Boy, when cancer got a hold of her it took her fast. He was there for her all the way to the end. They were quite a team. It's probably good for both of you to have some fun. You're both past due."

She looked at him and gave him a sarcastic smile. "It's just lunch."

"Yeah, sure." Zeke folded up his newspaper. "I have to go out for a while. I've had a call about a missing daughter and then I'm meeting Margie for an early lunch. If I'm running late, just lock things up."

* * * * *

The GPS directed Zeke to one of the older neighborhoods of Cincinnati. After a pleasant drive along streets lined with large old oak trees, he came to the address. "Nice neighborhood," he mused. Pumpkins and pots of mums led to the front door.

He could hear the chimes ring out after he pressed the doorbell. An attractive woman dressed in jeans and a rust-colored sweater, who appeared to be in her mid-50s, opened the door.

"You must be Mr. Bailey," she said with a brief smile. "You're right on time." She made a hand gesture to welcome him into her home. A front hall table held wedding pictures—of the missing daughter, he presumed.

"Can I offer you coffee or tea?" she asked as they went into the living room.

"No thanks, I'm coffee'd out. I had my quota back at the office. So, tell me, what's going on with your daughter?"

"Well, she isn't really missing in the true sense of the word. She told me she was going 'off the grid.'"

"But she didn't tell you where she was going?"

"Right. You see she's afraid of her ex-husband. He beat her up once. It was horrible. We helped her get a lawyer and take him to court." She reached into a drawer in the table next to her and withdrew a manila envelope. Zeke took it from her outstretched hand and pulled out its contents; pictures of her daughter taken at a hospital. The glossies depicted a black swollen eye and bruises across her face and neck.

"Her husband just got out of jail a couple of months ago. It seems he's threatened her with violence somehow. She wouldn't tell me anything and begged me not to call the police. Charlie always seemed so sweet and well-mannered. We gave them a beautiful wedding and helped them settle in a cute little house. Everything seemed perfect. We just can't believe we didn't see through him. Meg said she would get in touch with me when she could, but wouldn't tell me anything else. It's been two months and I haven't heard a word from her." She began to dab at the tears welling up in her eyes.

He took out a little notebook and jotted a few things down. "You don't have any thoughts about where she might have gone?"

Mrs. Watkins shifted in her chair. "None. She was so afraid. She wouldn't have gone anywhere that I might think of."

Zeke looked up at his client. "What make of car does she drive? How about her cell phone?"

"She said she wasn't taking her phone for fear of being tracked. She didn't take her car either for the same reason." Mrs. Watkins began to cry. "I... I just don't know what to do. I just never thought something like this could happen to us."

"Do you have her cell phone?"

She dabbed her eyes again with a tissue. "No. I don't know where it is."

Zeke tried to be reassuring. "Well, there are a few things I can do. First, I'll need a current picture of her, the more recent the better. I'll check out train and bus stations, car rental agencies, places like that. Where did your daughter work?"

"She was a teacher, second grade, but she gave her notice before she left. The administration wasn't very happy about it. She didn't give them much time to replace her before the start of the new school year."

He stood up to leave and gave her the standard pitch. "Try not to worry too much. These things usually work out. She may be over-reacting. In the meantime, I'll check things out and keep an eye on her ex. I think I can locate him through the courts, assuming he has a parole officer. If you do hear from Meg, let me know. Do you have a picture of her I can use?"

"There's one in the hall." She led him to the front door. The table in the foyer held a variety of pictures from every stage of her missing child's life. She took one from a frame and handed it to him. "This is the most recent. It was taken for the school yearbook."

He looked down at the photo of a lovely young woman with long dark hair and a bright smile. "Thanks, this will help. I'll stay in touch." He walked to the door and turned to her. "Try not to worry. I'll call you the minute I find anything out, okay?"

"Yes, thank you, Mr. Bailey."

Clare Watkins watched Zeke get in his car and drive away. She returned to the hall table and gently picked up Meg's wedding picture. She carried it into the living room where she sat in a chair, she cradled it, held it to her face and began to cry. With the flood of tears came a flood of memories of Meg's beautiful wedding.

She remembered how much fun they had planning the wedding. They never disagreed about a thing. Clare decided it was Meg's wedding and she would have things the way she wanted. It was a whirlwind of paging through bridal magazines, tasting dishes for the dinner menu, shopping for bridesmaid dresses and for Meg's honeymoon. Clare remembered how close they became through the flurry of parties and bridal showers. What an exciting time it was taking part in a wedding that was every mother's dream for her daughter.

She just couldn't believe this was happening to her beautiful daughter. Clare knew she wasn't a perfect mother, but she did her best. She sat on the sidelines and cheered at Meg's soccer games, sat through ballet and piano lessons and even volunteered as a leader for Meg's Girl Scout troop.

She remembered sewing little blue tutus for Meg's dance recitals and stitching her merit badges on her Girl Scout sash, loving every minute of her life with her precious child.

How did it end up like this: Meg, a battered wife on the run? What had her mother's instinct missed. She delved deep into her memory for signs that Charlie could become violent with Meg, but there just weren't any. Maybe they didn't let him share his own opinions with them, but he never seemed to disagree with the things they did.

He was always agreeable. When she and Meg found their first home, which was located nearby, he was as excited about it as they were. Clare recalled the move and how much fun they had decorating the new house. All Clare needed to make life perfect was a grandchild. Now, she was relieved that there were no children involved.

She blew her nose and wiped her tears. "I've got to get myself together before Ed gets home from work," she said to herself. Her husband, like Clare, was holding himself together by a very thin thread. *At least,* Clare thought, *I will have some positive steps we're taking to find our child.* She went into the kitchen to see what she could serve for dinner tonight. She wasn't really hungry, and Ed didn't seem to have much of an appetite lately, but it was something to keep her mind busy, her body in motion.

* * * * *

Zeke tuned his car radio to his favorite blues station. He had seen so much abuse of women during his time as a police detective. The photo of Meg haunted him, another bright-eyed girl who had her whole future ahead of her.

His thoughts traveled on to his new assistant, Gwen. Although she never went into the fine details, Zeke suspected she had gone through abuse far worse than the pictures Meg's mother had shown him. There was something so vulnerable about his new employee. She was such a natural beauty he couldn't help noticing her in the morning. She was the proverbial beam of sunshine in his dreary day. He worried that he offended her with his compliments. He began to feel like a relic, what with the "Me Too" movement and all that women's rights stuff. He vowed to be more careful with Gwen because he didn't want to lose her.

Things were much more complicated nowadays. Zeke felt relieved that his own son and daughter were grown and happy, even though they were on the other side of the country. After Margie retired from teaching at the local high school, she began trying to convince him to take early retirement from the police force. She had always supported him in his career. He knew how much she worried over the years, especially after his heart attack, so he eventually decided to take her up on retiring. For a few years they traveled back and forth across the country to visit their children and grandchildren, but soon realized their kids had a life of their own. Zeke began to get restless. There weren't enough leaky faucets, touch-up paint jobs or yard projects to fill his empty days. Margie wasn't thrilled when he decided to open the agency, but she relented when he argued that he could make his own hours and, if he wanted, close down for a week or two so they could travel.

Margie had told him to meet her at Garbo's, a restaurant near where she was playing bridge with a group of retired teachers today and on his way back to the office. She was waiting in a booth by the window and stood up and waved to him as he entered.

"How did it go?" his wife asked as he sat down and looked at the menu.

Zeke sighed. "Okay, I guess. There's nothing worse than being face to face with a parent of a missing child. Her daughter looks so much like our own Debbie—the same bright eyes and long dark hair. It brought up all of the ways I worried about Debbie, especially when she went gaga over that jerk in her senior year. Thank God that relationship didn't last. My experience tells me this missing girl situation isn't going to have a happy ending."

The collage of silent-movie stars on the face of the menu reflected the restaurant's theme. "I think I'll have the Keystone Kops. How about you?" He looked into the crystal blue eyes that had been twinkling back at him ever since he met her on a blind date more years ago than he cared to count. For Zeke it was love the first time he took her into his arms under the lights twinkling over the dance floor. They slow danced to the old Nat King Cole ballad "Stay as Sweet as You Are." It became their song. Mary Margaret Flannigan, his Irish beauty, who had always walked beside him no matter what life threw their way, was still as sweet as she was that night.

"Zeke, you know you should be eating something more sensible." Margie frowned just as their waitress approached the table. "I think I'll have The Grand Hotel," his wife told the waitress, who was dressed as a movie theater usherette from the silent movie era.

"Keystone Kops for me," Zeke said, ignoring Margie's frown. "They sure go all out for this 'silent movies' theme." He hated these trendy restaurants Margie and her friends enjoyed. *Just give me a greasy chili parlor*, he thought.

"I think it's kind of cute." Margie took a sip of her iced tea. "It reminds me of that little neighborhood restaurant we used to go to when we were first married. Remember how my parents loved to go there with us? They were so proud to be seen with a young rookie policeman, especially an Irish one."

"Yeah, I do remember, but I don't see any resemblance to this place."

Their food arrived and Zeke began to fill his wife in on the case of the missing daughter. "I keep thinking about Debbie and how awful it would be if something like this was going on in her life. I am also thinking about some of the horrible things I saw when I was on the force. None of it bodes well. I sure hope I can find this girl before it's too late."

Margie picked up her fork like a weapon and pointed at Zeke. "I hate to harp on it, but why don't you just give it all up, Zeke? This worry isn't good for you. You have to remember you're not as young as you used to be. You need to think more about your health. Or have you forgotten what it was like to wake up in a hospital hooked up to all kinds of machinery." Margie removed the tiny paper hotel from the top of her Grand Hotel salad and dug her fork into the lettuce with a vengeance.

"C'mon, Margie. My last doctor's visit was great."

"Okay, I give up. I give up." She put her hands up as if in surrender. "So, how's your new hire doing? What's her name, Gwen?"

"She's great. I'm afraid I offend her sometimes when I comment on how she looks. I told you she's been through two abusive marriages."

Margie let out a sigh in exasperation. "Zeke, when are you going to jump into the twenty-first century? I know you mean well, but don't comment on women's appearances at the office. You can be such a relic!"

"I just told myself the same thing coming over here in the car." He bit into his bun filled with sausage and kraut.

Margie put down her fork and grabbed his hand. "You know how I love old things," she whispered as she thought of how she almost lost him to a heart attack. "But you have to take care of old relics, Zeke. By the way, Debbie called this morning. She's planning on coming with her family over the Christmas holidays. I haven't heard from Gary yet, but I'm pretty sure they'll be coming home, too."

Zeke smiled. "There's nothing like a house full of kids over the holidays. I guess that means the shopping and cooking is about to begin. Do you have any ideas about gifts?"

"They've both e-mailed me with the children's lists, and I thought we could give Debbie and Gary and their spouses a night on the town together with free babysitting included."

Zeke smiled at the images of Christmas in his mind. Margie loved to decorate the house, make cookies and plan the traditional meals. "As soon as Thanksgiving is over, I'll bring the Christmas decorations down from the attic. We'll have to get them their annual new ornament to hang on the tree. Maybe plan a night at the Zoo Festival of Lights, they love that. It'll be a lot of fun. And, as much as I love them, there's nothing like putting our feet up and snuggling in front of the fire after they go home." Margie smiled and nodded in agreement.

He glanced at his watch. "Well, I better get back to the office so that Gwen can take a break. She has a lunch date with Jack Manley."

"Jack Manley! That's so nice. He's the one whose wife died of cancer a few years back isn't he? It would be so nice if they would get together. I'm sure he's very lonely."

"I'm quoting Gwen here: 'It's just lunch.'" Zeke picked up their check and signaled their waitress.

"I'm off to my bridge game. See you tonight, honey." Margie picked up her purse, gave him a quick peck on the cheek and headed for the door. He watched her leave and thought about how lucky he was to have her. Zeke realized he wasn't the easiest husband to live with.

As he sat at a traffic light on the main thoroughfare tapping his fingers on the steering wheel to the beat of the music, Zeke noticed a farmer's market stand with a vibrant display of orange and purple mums similar to the ones he admired on Clare Watkin's front porch. He turned the car into the lot, thinking, *I think I'll take some home to my Margie.*

* * * * *

Jack and Gwen went to lunch at a local Italian restaurant known for designer pizzas. They both ordered, he with anchovies, she without. Gwen began to relax in the warm environment; the buzz of workers on their lunch hour, the slight smell of garlic and the happy Italian music playing in the background.

"I hope things are looking better for you today."

She felt the genuine concern in Jack's voice. "I'm much better. I still think there is more to her death than it appears." She went into the details she knew so far.

"Did you say her ex-husband was Judge Kildeer?"

"Yes, do you know him?"

"Who doesn't? He's one of the richest men in the tri-state area. He comes from a long line of senators and representatives who took advantage of insider trading. His granddaddy invested in property with advance knowledge of where the exits on the interstate highway would be located. How do you think all of those senators become millionaires while they serve in Washington?" Jack picked up a bread stick and started to munch on it. "I had a few cases in Kildeer's court. He has a great record, but he's known for passing out tough sentences. He has a reputation for being a bit quirky. Everything in his court-room has to be in perfect order, right up to the jury chairs being in perfect alignment."

A man who was following a waiter to the back of the dining room waved to Jack. He returned the wave.

"One of my clients," he explained. "Where were we? Oh, yes. I wouldn't put too much stock in what your friend's sister says. Remember, she's grieving."

"That's what my boss says."

"Well, Zeke knows his stuff. Probably a good idea to listen to his advice."

Gwen didn't care what they said. She knew something wasn't right with the whole thing. "He said he worked with you and your wife when you had a law practice."

"Yes, Kay really liked him. She was a good judge of character."

There was an awkward pause.

"I am sorry, I don't know how to act on a date anymore, but I am sure talking about my deceased wife is not a good move."

Gwen reddened. "Oh, is this a date?" She smiled. "I thought it was just a lunch."

"Consider it a date. So, tell me about yourself." Jack filled their glasses with water from the pitcher that had been placed on their table.

Suddenly Gwen was spilling out her life story. She usually waited some time to reveal her past, since it was difficult. She told him about getting pregnant at 16 and, at the insistence of both sets of parents, getting married. She described the narrow-minded small town where she grew up and the local tavern her father owned. They lived upstairs. Everyone knew everyone and they all attended the same church. It was out of the question for her to have a baby out of wedlock and for him to shirk his responsibilities. He listened intently as she told him about the night she lost her baby. She didn't go into her second marriage in any detail. The first one was horrible enough to relive. All she said was that he was abusive. "One of the things I am working through, is why did I pick them."

The strains of joyful Italian music in the background, as if on cue, turned to a soulful ballad.

Jack put his hand on top of hers. "I'm so sorry you've been through so much."

"Well, I'll be very careful the next time. If there is a next time."

"Any man who abuses women is a real jerk."

Gwen was relieved to see the waiter approach them with their order. He was just in time to change the subject.

"Let's dig in, it looks great!" Jack served them each a steaming slice.

Gwen screwed up her face. "Ugh, I'll never understand how anyone can tolerate anchovies."

He took a big bite and smiled. "Maybe that's what was wrong with your exes, they didn't eat anchovies."

She laughed and realized how easy it was to be with him.

When they finished lunch he took her into his travel agency and introduced her to his co-workers. Gwen felt very uncomfortable under their scrutiny. It felt like being brought home to the meet the family.

Jack led her to his cluttered desk and reached through the stacks of brochures. He handed her one on the Galapagos Islands. "My favorite place in the world."

She glanced through the booklet that displayed pristine islands, wildlife in its natural habitat, sea lions, turtles, rare birds and beautiful aqua ocean waters. "It looks beautiful, so exotic. I'd be happy to get to Chicago at this point."

"Well, that is an easy wish to fill." He grinned. "Oops. I'm sorry, I think I'm moving too fast."

"Just a tad." Gwen glanced at the clock on the wall. "I have to get back to work." She put down the brochure and picked up her handbag. "Thanks for a great lunch, I really enjoyed it."

As the elevator ascended, she began to regret telling him so much about her past. Gwen wondered what he would think about someone who had so much baggage. She entered the office feeling very vulnerable, a feeling she didn't like.

5
MAURA

She studied her reflection in the cracked, dingy mirror. *Typical bar restroom,* she thought as she leaned in to apply a fresh coat of Siren Red lipstick. She loved her new look. She wore straight, bottle-blonde hair and heavy, stylish makeup. Her bright red knit dress stuck to her body like glue. Ralph wouldn't let her wear anything even close to this. He was so insanely jealous. If she tried to look the least bit sexy, he would go into a rage and slap her silly.

She massaged her sore left collarbone, a souvenir of the last and final time Ralph beat her up. With the help of a women's advocate and an attorney she made him pay big time. It would take a lot of hauls in his semi to pay her off. Maura's life had been one big party since her move to Chicago. She was making up for all of those years stuck at home watching him drink Jack Daniels until he lapsed into oblivion. At long last she was free!

Maura's thoughts went to the great guy she met right here at the Bee Hive Bar and Grill. He had bought her a drink a few nights ago and every night since. He seemed really nice and very easy to talk to. He, too, had just ended a bad marriage and was looking for companionship. Tonight he had asked to take her home. Maura knew he probably wanted more than companionship and that was okay. She was ready for some good sex. She blotted her lipstick and smiled at herself in the mirror, placed the gold tube back into her bag, threw the tissue into the overflowing trash basket and went out to join the gorgeous hunk of a man waiting outside the door.

He stood up as she returned to the table. "Are you ready to go?" he asked. He put his muscular arms around her and kissed her on the neck and throat, his tongue arousing every fiber of her being.

"Am I ever," she smiled and pressed against him, her body throbbing to be fulfilled. "Let's go to my place, Max."

6
'LOOK OUT, GWENNIE'

By week's end Gwen knew she needed to attend her meeting. She was having more and more nightmares about her abuse. She also couldn't get her friend Julia out of her thoughts. And then there was Jack Manley, who managed to be near the door of his agency every morning when she arrived at work, waving and smiling as she waited for the elevator. She wasn't ready for a relationship; wasn't sure she ever would be.

The group was large, but she managed to talk about her nightmares, which prompted other participants to share theirs. Gwen realized these dreams were a form of PTSD.

Jen called to her as she was getting into her car to leave. "Hey, Gwen, did you talk to your boss about Julia's sister's phone call?"

"Yes, I did. He thinks I'm overreacting. But I feel it in my bones that something isn't right."

Jen leaned against Gwen's car. "That's how I feel. I can't get her out of my mind. I guess when someone so beautiful and vibrant is killed it's hard to accept. What makes matters even worse, I attended a luncheon with a professional group I belong to. One of my associates is going through a similar thing. One of her attendees went off to Chicago to start a new life and was found beaten and strangled in her apartment. What a horrible stroke of bad luck."

Gwen gasped. "Do they know who did it?"

"Evidently she was seen several nights in a row at a local bar with a man and was seen leaving the bar with him that night. But there was no crime scene evidence, and they haven't found the guy who did it yet." Jen stepped away from Gwen's car. "Well, I'm off, I've got an early appointment tomorrow." She tapped the side of Gwen's car with her hand. "Be careful out there."

Gwen's mind raced on the drive home. Another woman who was starting over, dead. She had visions of the woman in the bar drinking and having fun, perhaps thinking the worst part of her life, the abuse, was behind her. She was starting over. Then she had horrible visions of the women being beaten and strangled. Gwen saw a red light just in time and slammed on her brakes to avoid going through it. The person behind the wheel in the next lane looked over and shook his head. "I've got to put this out of my mind," she told herself as she took a deep breath.

Gwen went home and forced herself into her usual routine. Kick off the heels, feed Ethel, pour a glass of Merlot and curl up on the sofa. Her phone was turned off during the meeting. She turned it on and checked for messages. There was a text from Jack. **How about lunch again tomorrow? I'll see you at the elevators.**

"Look out, Gwennie," she thought. "You're really not ready for this."

She went to sleep, dreaming about Julia and the dead girl in Chicago and the men who had ruined her life.

7
MAX

He gave himself a final once-over in the full-length mirror, thinking, *I'm the master of disguise.* He smiled approvingly at his new reflection.

His suitcases were on the bed, packed for a nice vacation in Hilton Head where he was looking forward to some sun and a little golf. The money had been in the safe deposit box just as planned.

The next phase was for him to lie low for a while, maybe a month until the next item on the agenda, whoever she might be. Meanwhile he planned on living the high life for a while. This was such easy money. It almost made him laugh.

The hotel valet knocked on the door, and at Max's direction, grabbed the packed luggage and escorted him to the hotel entrance where he called for a limo. Max basked in the luxury of the hotel lobby; the brass fixtures, the fresh orchids, the gleaming marble floors; a far cry from some of the real shitholes he had slept in as an agent.

He sat back in the leather seat of the limo catching his reflection in the rearview mirror. The short blond haircut certainly did the trick. "Yes, I am the master of disguise," he mused to himself.

As they crawled along in traffic a bus crept along beside them, displaying a colorful ad for Army recruitment. The soldier on the banner looked just like his father: square-jawed, dark hair and deep blue eyes. It was the image of the father he never knew, whose picture graced their fireplace mantle alongside the framed gold star. He was killed in action during the last days of the Vietnam War. Max's mother never got over it. Their entire living room was a shrine to his memory.

His mother would tell anyone who would listen that Max was the spitting image of his father. She constantly told him he should grow up to be exactly like the dead hero. It was clear to him, even as a little child, that the only way he could win her love was to become just like his father. From a very early age he became what was expected of him regardless of the opposite feelings that found a harbor below the surface. Max learned to suppress those feelings and became known in their middle-class, rural Indiana neighborhood as the good kid, the one who would stand up for the underdog on the playground. He excelled in school, joined the Boy Scouts and rose to the rank of Eagle Scout. He groomed himself to be a superhero.

Max achieved a partial scholarship to the University of Cincinnati, where he joined a fraternity and developed friendships that would advance his plans for the future. He joined ROTC in order to pay for the rest of his education. It all led to a stint in the Army and that led to being recruited by the CIA. He was the good guy. He became one of their top agents. One they could send anywhere, knowing he would slay the dragons and keep the homeland safe from the forces of evil. When his mother succumbed to kidney disease, she died believing that she had raised a good son whose father would be proud of him. She had done a good job as a mother.

But then there was the incident in Ankara, where he crossed the line one too many times and was brought back. A whistleblower, probably that bitch female agent they sent to join him in the field, reported him. It was because he pushed the envelope that the enemy was vanquished. He'd seen the horrific ways they tortured prisoners. If we wanted to win, we had to be as vicious as they were. He, the master of subterfuge, the agent they could send anywhere to get the job done, was demoted to a boring desk job. He couldn't believe "the company" could be so short sighted. What did invisible lines matter as long as the enemy was destroyed?

During that year, the one he thought of as his year in exile, there was another betrayal. His wife of 15 years sued for divorce. His marriage had become so weakened by his long absences and her constant worrying that she had found another man and wanted out. He wasn't all that surprised. It had become more a marriage of convenience, part of his stateside façade. Sex with her was obligatory, at best. He had become used to another type of woman—the kind that hung around bars near army bases and would do just about anything you wanted for a few extra bucks. Because of the two women who betrayed him, one at the CIA and one on the domestic front, he found himself in alien territory. He moved out of their high-priced condo in Alexandria and rented an apartment in Bethesda where the rent was a little cheaper. He didn't mind living alone and he could get sex anytime he wanted, but it gnawed at him that his wife had replaced her perfect husband like a worn-out pair of shoes.

He longed for the excitement, the adventure, the slaying of the dragon. Max knew sooner or later something would break his way. His reputation preceded him. His patience eventually paid off. A friend from his early days in the CIA called and wanted to meet him for dinner to discuss a possible career move.

They met at a popular steakhouse in D.C. Max was wired, feeling again the electric buzz that preceded a new assignment. After catching up on the intervening years, his friend John got to the point.

"I'm recruiting for a new firm. I heard through the grapevine about you being pulled back in. Really bad judgment on the part of the brass. Since the attack on nine-eleven we need every good man we've got to fight the war on terror." John slowly poured them another glass of expensive wine.

Max leaned forward. "I'm listening. Tell me about this new firm."

John began to speak in a lower, more secretive tone. "It's called OCTOPUS, which stands for Organization for Covert Tactical

Operations to Protect the United States. We will have tentacles that reach around the globe. We're located in the foothills of the Ozarks. We've developed a private army that the government has hired to operate in international war zones. We are setting up our own base and we have almost reached our goal of fifteen thousand troops at the ready. Our forces will be capable of overthrowing governments, if necessary, in the war on terror. We know of your stellar record and are willing to offer you a very good salary to lead operations in Afghanistan and Iraq."

Max's heart was jumping around in his chest. Finally, someone appreciated his abilities.

He didn't care about the salary they were offering, although the number John wrote on a napkin was much more than he was earning at the CIA. He jumped at the chance to get back into the game.

For the next three years he led the undercover operations in the war arena. He trained his teams to be ruthless in achieving the mission, just as he was. He realized that what he missed the most sitting at a desk wasn't the excitement or the adventure; it was the kill, the feeling of power that came over him when his prey realized they were about to die.

It all came to an abrupt end when the Afghan government disapproved of one of their missions. Twenty-one civilians were mistakenly slaughtered, and a complaint was made to a U.S. senator on the foreign relations committee who had been backing them. The Afghanis threatened to go public about the secret army. They were pulled out within six months. OCTOPUS eventually had to temporarily shut down. The owners and backers were trying to regroup under another name and get back into the war business again. Max laid low, hoping they would reopen soon, but a year went by and no word.

That's when he received a phone call from an old fraternity brother. He smiled as he remembered the call while the limo driver dodged through the bumper-to-bumper traffic on the way to O'Hare Airport.

Finally, they pulled up to "Departures" and Max's luggage was handed off to the check-in valet. Max tipped them each generously, saying, "Life is good. Life is good."

ANNETTE LACKNER

8
CONSIDER IT A DATE

She drove her Camry through the streets of Cincinnati, marveling at what a beautiful fall day it was. The leaves were in their full glory and the sun was shining from a vibrant blue sky. Everything had a clean, brand new feeling to it. When she parked in the lot behind the Arnold Building, she saw Jack getting out of a red Mazda Miata. She smiled and waved.

"Good morning," he called. She waited as he approached her, trying not to appear too anxious to see him. "Did you get my message about lunch?"

"I sure did." They walked side by side to the front of the building.

"Well, I've got a better idea. How about dinner tonight? And consider it a date."

She hesitated for a moment and then thought about another night with Ethel and the Merlot. "Sure, that sounds nice." She told herself it's just dinner and she could walk away from him anytime she wanted.

Jack smiled. "It's such a gorgeous day, I thought maybe we could go somewhere down on the riverfront. It won't be long before it will be too cold. What do you think? Maybe the Boat House?"

She smiled at the thought. "I'm putty in your hands. I love ribs. Are you thinking of going straight from work?" Her mouth watered just thinking of a beautiful slab of ribs.

"Sure, that much more daylight to enjoy." They passed through the revolving doors and stopped in front of Far Horizons.

"Can you be off by five? I'll make reservations." Jack pushed the elevator button for her.

"Sounds like a plan." She waved good-bye noticing the gazes of his co-workers through the glass. "What am I doing?" she asked herself. "I am not ready for this." However, another night watching TV with Ethel wasn't as appealing as sitting outside looking over the Ohio River. And she had to admit, not as appealing as spending an evening with Jack.

Zeke was in his usual fog behind the newspaper. He looked out at her and forgot his resolution to stop making personal comments. "You look nice today, a little more understated than usual. Got another date?"

"I wouldn't know how to start my day without your fashion commentary. Good deduction, gumshoe. I have a dinner date. Now can I get to work?" She tried to ignore him.

"With Jack Manley?" He smiled like the Cheshire cat.

"Yes, with Jack Manley." She could feel herself redden as she opened the file on her desk.

Gwen went over and opened a window. "If you don't quit smoking in here, you're going to get us thrown out."

"Nah, they're desperate for the rent. And other than cleaning people no one ever comes in here." He folded the paper and started to go through a stack of files that covered his desk.

Gwen saw an opening. "Zeke, I know you think I'm overreacting, but I've heard that another woman who was recovering from abuse and left town to start over was murdered in Chicago. Doesn't that seem like more than a coincidence? Two women within several weeks?"

Zeke closed a manilla folder. "Was she in your group?"

"No. A different one, but in Cincinnati."

"How was she killed?" Zeke walked over and sat in the chair next to her desk.

Maybe I finally have his attention, Gwen thought as she continued. "She left a bar with a stranger and was found beaten and strangled. So much for starting over."

"Gwen," Zeke started to talk in his most fatherly voice. "That's not even in the same state as your friend Julia. Chicago can be a very dangerous place if you're not careful. And, might I add, going home from a bar with a stranger isn't the smartest thing to do. You're asking for trouble when you do something like that. I think the deaths were a coincidence and I think if you really thought about it, you would too."

"You're probably right. I'll drop it, Zeke." Just then the phone rang and Zeke returned to his desk, answering with his usual, "Bailey here."

Gwen started going through yesterday's mail. She still didn't think it was just a coincidence; there was more here than met the eye.

* * * * *

They were glad the restaurant wasn't as crowded as usual. The Reds season was over and there were no big events in town. They had a table by a window and watched the sunset on the Ohio River, followed by the shimmering lights from the Kentucky side. Dinner was divine, as expected. The couple dug into the large slabs of ribs with gusto.

Jack said, "Thank God for the bibs they supply. I haven't yet mastered the art of stain removal. I haven't mastered the art of laundry at all. You've got barbecue sauce on your chin." He dipped his napkin in his water, reached over and wiped her chin, lingering a little longer than necessary, gazing into her eyes. "There, that's much better."

They ate until they were stuffed, passing on dessert.

As they left the restaurant Jack gave her a gentle poke with his elbow. "There's your friend."

Gwen gazed ahead to see an impeccably dressed middle-aged man getting into a chauffeured limousine. She threw Jack a questioning look.

"Judge Kildeer. Nothing but the best when you've got money. Let's walk."

Gwen wished she had gotten a better look at Julia's ex, but decided to push him out of her mind and enjoy the evening.

They strolled along the river walk, stepping aside occasionally for skateboarders and joggers to pass. It was a beautiful warm night and Gwen had to admit to herself that she was more than pleased when he held her hand. They discussed their lives, their heartbreaks, and Jack revealed he had a 20-year-old son who was away at college. Gwen put thoughts of the complications that might entail on the back burner.

"It gets pretty lonely with him away at school. I mean I have a lot of friends and keep busy, I work out regularly and play poker and golf with the guys, but I still feel so alone. I just rattle around in the house. I've thought about putting it on the market, but then I realize it is the only home Joe has ever known. I guess I'll hang on to it until Joe is completely on his own."

Gwen wondered what his home looked like. Did it reflect his late wife Kay's personality? "I know how it is. I feel pretty lonely myself sometimes. Although being married wasn't so great either."

Jack stopped and put his hands on her shoulders, turning her to face him.

"Look, I want to be honest with you. I was pretty low that day you ran into me, but there is something so refreshing about you. You lit a spark I thought was burned out forever. I know you're gun shy and I understand, but I would like to have a relationship with you. Just think about it. We can take our time. I am not in a hurry. Do I have a chance?"

Gwen was taken aback by his honesty. "It's not *if* you have a chance, but do you *want* to take a chance with a two-time loser like me."

He put his arms around her and kissed the top of her head. "You aren't the loser, they are. But what do you expect from jerks who don't eat anchovies? Come on, let's walk. I have to work off all of those ribs."

When they returned to the Arnold Building parking lot, he walked her to her Camry. He kissed her goodnight and even though it was a gentle kiss, it made her want more.

"The holiday season is coming up. It sure would be nice to have someone to share it with me. Think about it." He opened her door and kissed her again. Then he winked and walked away.

Ethel was more than a little put out about her dinner being late. She jumped on the counter and edged along the bottle of Merlot a bit confused that Gwen wasn't opening it.

"Not tonight," Gwen cooed, "Not tonight." She performed her nightly routine and slid into bed to a blessedly dreamless sleep.

*　*　*　*　*

When she arrived at work the next morning, she glanced into the travel agency. Jack was sitting with an older couple surrounded by travel brochures. Suddenly, he looked up and smiled at her. When she got on the elevator he was still looking, and she waved back.

"How was the date?" Zeke asked, as she closed the office door.

"Great, we went out for ribs and took a walk along the river."

"My Margie would consider that very romantic. Very romantic indeed." He stood up and grabbed a notebook. "I have to take off. Can you manage things here?"

"Of course. More work on the missing daughter?" She was hoping something interesting was in the air. This detective stuff was pretty boring so far.

"Yeah. Lots of legwork." He put on his rumpled jacket and smoothed down his sparse hair. "I don't have a good feeling about this one. I'll see what I can find out."

She watched her boss leave the office and started to update his computer contact file.

When she got to the "M's" she came to Manley, Jack and Kay. Behind Kay's name was written the word "deceased." She wondered about this deceased Kay. She knew she was a lawyer, probably very smart and elegant: nothing like Gwen. But Jack called Gwen "refreshing." Maybe he, too, was looking for something different, a way forward from the heartbreaking past. She allowed herself to think about what he might be planning for the holidays.

9
MEG

She put the finishing touches on the chicken casserole and lowered it into the oven. Meg loved this old house in rural Michigan. It had taken the last two months to adjust to living here, away from all she knew and loved. Her old college roommate Carly was so supportive. When Meg showed up at her front door, after hitching rides all of the way, she was greeted with open arms where she immediately collapsed into sobs of relief.

Carly helped her take off her backpack, sat Meg down and made her a cup of coffee, then listened in horror as Meg poured out her story. When she was notified that Charlie was released from prison, the memories of how he became so violent sent her into survival mode. She found herself jumping when the phone rang, always double checking the locks, listening at every little sound, looking into her rearview mirror. It happened so unexpectedly. She went to the local grocery store to pick up a few things after work. Just as she turned into the breakfast food aisle, she sensed his presence, the smell of his cologne, and there he was lurking behind her. "Long time no see." He ran his fingers through her hair and down her neck. "You're looking good, girl."

His warm breath on her neck made her skin crawl. "Stay away from me," she said, but as she started to push forward, he grabbed her upper arm.

"Just thought I would give you a little heads up. Sooner or later, you won't be looking so good. I have big plans for you."

ANNETTE LACKNER

An elderly man pushing a cart glanced over as he passed by. She
lurched forward trying to catch up, thinking if she kept in his sight
Charlie wouldn't harm her. She went through the checkout trying to
catch sight of her ex-husband, but he had disappeared. She decided
to call the police as soon as she got to her car.

Meg cautiously made her way out to the parking lot, trying to stay
near other people. Opening the trunk, she unloaded her groceries and
suddenly, there he was unloading them right beside of her as if the last
few years had never taken place.

"If you don't leave me alone, I'll call the police." She backed away,
placing her thumb over the horn symbol on her keypad.

He leaned against the car with a sneer on his face. "I don't think
that's such a good idea. It won't be me. I have friends, new friends. If
you even think about going to the police, I can't be responsible for
what happens to those precious parents of yours. What would you do
without Mommy and Daddy to fix things for you?"

As Meg finished her story Carly put down her coffee, astonished.
"There must be something you can do. The police surely can do something about this."

"But he said it wouldn't be him. He said he has friends. I can't take
a chance with my parents' safety."

Carly invited her to stay there for as long as she needed to. They
finally decided that Meg could be a sort of nanny for Carly's little boy.
She could certainly use the help. Since her young husband was killed
in Afghanistan it was really getting difficult to juggle the housework,
her nursing career and her little boy, Eli. And she was very lonely.

Meg changed her appearance. She bleached her hair and had it cut
into a shorter hairdo.

The two young women laughed remembering all of the crazy hair-
dos they experimented with when they were in school. They decided
on a new name for her: Audrey. They were both big Audrey Hepburn

fans. When they were roommates, they watched all of her movies over and over. The young women picked up right where they left off rekindling their friendship. They were now a team.

Meg smiled remembering that day a few months ago as she began making a green salad to finish off the meal. She glanced out from the kitchen window as she washed the lettuce. There was a man standing across the street staring at the house. Her heart began to pound as she backed away from the sink. Charlie's words echoed in her ears. "I have friends. It won't be me." Her body could almost feel his hands easing down her throat, smell his cologne. Staying out of sight, she reached across the counter to the knife block. She grabbed a butcher knife with her shaking hand and held it as she edged along the wall to the front door. After a minute or so, she finally mustered up enough courage to peek through the curtain on the door's window just as Carly was opening it. She screamed and dropped the knife.

"What's going on?" Carly screamed.

"There was a man across the street watching the house. Did you see him?" Meg hurried back to the wall trying to stay out of sight from the door's curtained window.

Carly pulled back the curtain and looked outside. "There is no one there now. It was probably just someone taking a walk. Lots of people stop and glance at this house. It's one of the few that has been completely restored. I think you're overreacting, Meg. Come on, let's sit you down." She took her trembling friend by the elbow and led her back into the kitchen.

"No, no, I'm okay. I know, you're probably right." Meg composed herself, replacing the knife and returning to the greens in the sink. "You're probably right, I'm just on edge. Eli is playing next door. He should be home any minute. I'll set the table while you freshen up." She took a deep breath and allowed the knot in her stomach to loosen.

"Are you sure you're okay?" Carly asked as she walked toward her bedroom.

"Yes, I'm good," she called back to her.

Meg tried to clear her mind and dared to glance out the window again. The tall blond man had vanished into the air as quickly as the dead November leaves.

10
SISTER TALK

She hated the time change. She drove home in a rainy darkness, typical of early November, which brought her spirits even lower than they already were. Jack had to go on a trip to check out some resorts in South America and had been gone for three weeks. She missed him terribly and at the same time hated that she missed him.

She and Ethel dined together: Gwen, a huge tossed salad created at the supermarket and Ethel, her usual tin of cat food. As Gwen cleaned up, Ethel rubbed against the bottle of Merlot in the wine holder. Gwen was reminded of her friend Julia's struggle with alcoholism. "Are you trying to make me an alcoholic? I've got enough problems. Just one glass, okay?" The cat rubbed against her hand as she uncorked and poured. "Let's get cozy."

Just as she sat down on the sofa and pulled a warm afghan across her lap, the phone rang. Gwen recognized her sister's number from Florida.

"Hi, Ali, how are you?" She pulled Ethel onto her lap and began petting the cat's silky coat.

"I'm good. Just thought I'd check in and see how you're doing. How's the new job?"

"It's okay. Not as exciting as I thought it would be, but it pays the bills. Actually, tomorrow I'll be outside doing surveillance. It will be a nice break from the four walls of the office. How's the weather in Naples?" Ethel began to purr loudly, somehow the sound comforted Gwen.

"Gorgeous, as usual. The real estate business has been going great guns, so I've been really busy. That's why I haven't called for a while."

Gwen pictured Ali sitting on the balcony of her condo, gazing out at the beautiful ocean waters. It made her dread the coming winter even more. "Well, that's a good thing. Right?"

"I guess so. I'm thinking about getting married again. Carl and I have decided to make it legal."

"That's great. It's about time. How many years have you been together, five or six?" Carl managed the real estate office where Ali worked. "Have you set a date?"

Ethel jumped from her lap and stretched out on a chair as Gwen took a slow sip of wine.

"Probably this spring. Are you seeing anyone? It's been three years."

"As a matter fact, I just met a really nice guy. We've been out to lunch and had a dinner date. I don't know, I don't think I'm ready. Too many battle scars. He's different than my exes. He's very gentle and kind, a bit of a nerd in a sweet way. He owns a travel agency in the lobby of the building where I work. I guess I just don't trust my own judgment anymore. He's almost too good to be true and you know what they say about things that seem too good to be true."

"Just go slow. You've got to quit feeling guilty about your marriages. After all, you were a sixteen-year-old kid who fell for a jock and got pregnant. What did you know about anything? I could still kill him for what he did to you. Our parents should never have insisted that the two of you get married. That damn small-town community we grew up in where everyone knew everyone and went to the same little church. It was okay for dad to beat up on mom, but they couldn't have an unmarried daughter with a child. I hope I never have to lay eyes on that hick town again!"

Gwen tightened her grasp on the wine glass in her hand, trying to push back the awful memory of a night so long ago. Their trailer was filled with the aroma of Bavarian sauerkraut. It was her first attempt to cook Mark's favorite dish. To this day, the pungent smell of kraut made Gwen sick to her stomach. She could see the door to their little trailer fly open and Mark storm in. "What do you mean calling me over and over while I'm out with the guys?" He threw his jacket across the room. "Can't you just leave me alone when I'm out?" He stumbled toward her.

"You could at least let me know if you aren't going to be here for dinner." She started to cry. "I've just been sitting here and worrying about you."

"I'm sitting here and worrying about you, waah, waah, waah," he mocked her. He was reeking with the smell of beer. "Get up and reheat the food, I'll eat it."

She started crying harder. He grabbed her by the arm and yanked her off the sofa. "Go reheat it, I said."

"Reheat it yourself!" she dared to scream back at him.

He grabbed her by the hair and dragged her into the kitchen. "I said, reheat it."

In a flash of rage, he was pulling dishes out of the refrigerator and slamming them on the stove. Gwen was crying hysterically.

"I SAID REHEAT THE DAMN FOOD!"

She started to run into the tiny bedroom to get away from him, but he caught her by the arm and threw her into the kitchen. She hit the edge of the table and fell across a chair. "Stop, please stop! The baby," she screamed as she tried to run for the door, but he overpowered her and started to slap her, over and over. Then the slaps turned into punches. With each blow, the pain became more and more unbearable.

When she came to in the hospital there was no baby and no more babies to come. Gwen felt like a hollow shell that had once held and nurtured a baby, and even though the pain of the hysterectomy, her cracked ribs and broken arm was horrific, the pain of knowing she could never have children cut much deeper. She was just what her father had said when he found out she was pregnant: "Used

Merchandise." She blamed herself for being stupid enough to fall for the star quarterback. The guy all of her girlfriends wanted to catch. She should not have given in to the desires he aroused in her. Her life was over. When her parents visited, her father said, "No one will want you now that you can't have kids." Gwen looked at her mother sitting in the green hospital chair holding her Bible and waited for her to say something, anything to defend her daughter, but as usual, she was the silent, subservient wife who lived in the book on her lap.

"Are you still there, Gwen?"

She was momentarily startled by the sound of Ali's voice on the other end of the line. "I shouldn't have argued with a drunk twice my size. I knew he used steroids to have an edge on the football field. I'd seen his aggressive behavior. I was so stupid. What was I thinking?"

Gwen could hear her sister's loud sigh through the phone. "You sound like Mom: 'I shouldn't have egged him on. I should have kept quiet.' They are responsible for what they did."

"I know you're right. That much I understand through my support group. We didn't have much of an example on how to stand up for ourselves did we? I feel like I'm just part of the viscous cycle."

She saw a blinking flash of red on her phone. "I have a call coming in. Can I call you back later?"

"Is it the nerd?" Ali cooed.

"It sure is."

She retrieved the call. "Hi, Jack. How are things in Ecuador?"

"Pretty good, lots of interesting things to do here. The hotel is really nice. I have a great view of downtown Quito. I just took a walk in the park across the street. It's full of iguanas. They are really fascinating to watch."

"Ugh, are they dangerous?"

"No more than the squirrels in the parks at home. What about you? What are you doing tonight?"

"Nothing much, just me and the cat having dinner. My sister just called from Florida to tell me she and her live-in boyfriend are going to get married this spring."

"Well, now I know more about you. I didn't know your sister lives in Florida, and I didn't know you have a cat. What's her name?"

"My sister is Ali, and my cat is Ethel."

"Ethel? What the heck kind of a name is that for a cat?"

"It's a perfectly wonderful name. Lucy had her 'partner in crime' and so do I."

"That brings back a lot of happy memories. I used to watch *I Love Lucy* re-runs with my mom after school. Mom was a big fan. So, I'm wondering if you're free Saturday night? I come home on Thursday. I thought we might go out to dinner."

Gwen walked over to the counter and poured herself another glass of wine. "My calendar is an empty space on Saturday. I'd love to."

*   *   *   *   *

Gwen picked up a cup of hot coffee from the fast-food restaurant where she could sit in her car to watch her subject from the parking lot. She took the precaution of locking her doors, knowing she was in a riskier part of town. She sipped on the warm black liquid and decided this was the most boring work in the world. She wondered where Jack wanted to go for dinner Saturday night and thought about shopping for something new to wear, even though she couldn't afford it. Suddenly she spotted the subject leaving his apartment. As he entered his car, she eased out into traffic so she could follow him from a couple cars behind. She followed him to a Home Fix It store and watched him park in the employee parking area. Well, his place of employment checked out. She waited about a half an hour and decided to go into the store. She strolled around glancing up and down aisles until she spotted him in the wall hangings area. He looked at her. "Can I help you with something?" She felt his eyes travel slowly from her head to toes. The name badge over his shirt pocket identified him as C H A R L I E. He was the guy.

Charlie was a big man who obviously worked out. His hair was cut in a buzz, which made his head look too small for his huge shoulders. His strong build reminded Gwen of Mark and she felt a little shiver when she remembered that this man was also an abuser.

"I'm looking for something to hang pictures on the wall. I just moved into a new apartment and don't have a clue as to what I'm doing. What's the best thing to use?"

"There are different kinds of hooks, depending on weight and so on. Look through these and I'll come back to see if you have any questions. I just got here, and they need me in another department. I'll be right back."

Gwen looked at her watch. "This is going to take a little longer than I thought. I have an appointment. If I come back about four will you still be here?" She flashed him a big smile.

"Sure, I am here until five-thirty."

"Great! I'll be back." She watched the suspect walk to the end of the aisle and disappear. She hurried back to the car and made a note in her phone. "Works till 5:30."

Gwen checked in with Zeke and gave him an update.

"You went in and engaged with him? My God, Gwen, don't ever let your subject see you, it's too dangerous."

"I'm sorry, I didn't think when I did it."

Zeke could hear the regret in her voice. "Don't worry about it. It was a rookie mistake. Shame on me for not warning you. All's okay."

There was a nice mall close by where she could shop for a dress. After a light lunch at a little café in the bookstore, she returned to a nearby discount shop and purchased a dark green knit dress with a V-neck. It brought out the green in her eyes. She even shopped for some new jewelry to wear with it, something she hadn't allowed herself to do in years.

As Gwen headed back to her car, she spied the Royal Headdress Salon just down the street. It was part of the chain she once worked for and her second husband owned. She immediately had a flashback of her last brutal night with him and walked out of her way to avoid passing it. She knew she was being silly. She heard through the grapevine he had moved to a gated golf community in Florida with his latest trophy on his arm; a beautiful young blonde he met at one of the salons. Supposedly he only came back to Cincinnati twice a year to check on his business operations. She still didn't want to take a chance of running into him. Seeing him might set her back in her recovery. She just wanted to think about going out to dinner with Jack. She had to keep moving forward with her life.

About 4:30 she drove through the Fix It Store's parking lot and noted that the subject's car was still there and made a note in her phone. The end of another monotonous day.

Gwen decided to go to her meeting, so she stopped and had a bite to eat and shopped a little more.

When the meeting went into session, she described the fear she felt when she walked out of her way to avoid passing a shop that was part of her second husband's hair salon chain. She also talked about her fears about starting a new relationship with Jack. It helped to put these thoughts out in the open.

Jen approached her after the room emptied and asked if there was any news about Julia and Maura. "The whole thing is just too strange," Jen said, waving to some of the participants as they left the building.

Gwen plunged her hand into her huge purse to retrieve her car keys. "I know. I think it's strange, too. Nothing has turned up on my end. How about you?"

Jen shook her head no. "I guess we just have to move on. How's your job going?"

Gwen sighed. "Now I'm tailing an abuser who has threatened his ex-wife. I just can't get away from these creeps. Well, I'll see you next time."

Gwen got in her car. "Another boring day, time to go home to Ethel and the Merlot."

11
INVITATION

Jack arrived at her apartment at 6:00 on the dot with a bouquet of red roses in one hand and an expensive looking wine in the other.

"I love roses," she said, inhaling the heavy fragrance. "Thank you. Come on in, I'm almost ready. Can I pour you a glass of wine?" Gwen couldn't understand why she was as nervous as a teen-ager going on a first date.

"That would be very nice. Wow! You look great in that dress. It brings out your green eyes." He followed her into the kitchen area and watched as she uncorked and poured the wine. "Don't I even get one little kiss as a welcome home?"

She looked up and smiled at him and put her hands on his shoulders. "Of course." She gave him an affectionate peck on the cheek.

"You must not have missed me as much as I missed you. I was thinking of something more like this." He took her into his arms and kissed her in a way that showed much deeper passion. Ethel, who had been hiding out of sight, jumped onto the counter and gave out a loud "MEOW."

Gwen burst into laughter. "I am so sorry! She's not used to having a man in her domain."

"Did you train her to do that?" Ethel rubbed against the wine bottle as she scrutinized Jack.

"Who, me?" Gwen took a crystal vase out of the cabinet, filled it with tap water and deposited the red roses into it. "I'll go finish getting ready. Have a seat."

Jack looked into Ethel's large yellow eyes and scowled. "Am I safe?"

"You never know," Gwen sang out from her bedroom as she placed her new necklace around her neck. She was so glad she chose this dress.

Jack had made reservations at a local restaurant known for delicious seafood entrees. The waitress escorted them to a corner booth for two, dimly lit and very romantic. A wine steward appeared with an expensive looking bottle of wine and poured a small amount into a glass. Jack sniffed it, swirled it a bit and then tasted. "Perfect."

"This is lovely. You've gone to quite a bit of trouble." Gwen placed the fine linen napkin across the folds of her dark green dress.

They toasted with the fine crystal wine glasses. "To the future," Jack said softly, looking into her eyes.

Gwen felt her entire body go limp. "To the future," she murmured.

He told her about his trip and the wonderful places he had seen. As Jack colorfully described places like Machu Pichu, a mountain resort in Otavallo and Lake Titicaca, Gwen found herself wondering what it would be like to explore those exotic sounding places with this tenderhearted man.

Over the Crème Brule, he asked her, "Do you have plans for Thanksgiving? It's next week in case you didn't know."

"No, I don't have plans. Ethel and I were going to do takeout. Don't tell me you're going to roast a turkey." She loved the way he slightly tilted his head to the left just before he broke into a huge grin.

"No, my son Joe goes to Northwestern. I was going to go up there to take him out for Thanksgiving dinner. I thought you might want to come along." He nervously pushed his glasses up on his nose. "I have an agency I want to visit while I'm there, but that will just take one day. I thought I would drive up on Tuesday night, take care of business on Wednesday and spend Thursday with Joe, then drive back on Friday or Saturday. What do you think?"

Gwen had a flashback to that waiting dinner many years ago—the rage, the pain, the loss.

She began to fiddle with her dessert fork. "Oh, Jack, I just don't know. I'm not sure I can miss work and honestly...."

"Honestly what?" He refreshed their wine.

"Well, the implications of being away in a hotel, I'm not sure if I'm ready for that."

He put his hand over her fidgeting one. "I'll get you a separate room if that would make you feel better. No *quid pro quo* expected. I'm not saying it wouldn't be nice, but as I told you, I'm not in a hurry. You can even lock your door, since your buddy Ethel won't be there to protect you. You told me you would like to go to Chicago."

"I did?"

"Yeah, when I was talking up the Galapagos you said, and I quote, 'I'd be happy just to get to Chicago.'"

"Oh, so you're going to throw that back at me. Something I said when I was upset." They laughed and left it at that.

When he brought her home, she invited him in for a nightcap. Ethel was lurking around their feet.

"I'll let you feed her. That will win her over."

Jack watched as she opened the tin and filled the little plastic bowl with the slimy looking contents. She handed it to Jack, who placed it on the kitty mat in the corner. Ethel sized him up and slowly approached her dinner. She looked at him again, blinked and then started to eat.

They took their drinks into the living room and sat next to each other on the sofa. As they sipped, Jack talked about his son and how he was finally getting used to the loss of his mother. He described to her some of the places to see and things to do in Chicago. The city of Chicago made Gwen think about the woman who was strangled in the bar. She immediately changed the subject.

"How are you able to make it in the travel business? I thought everyone made their own reservations online now."

"Well, I specialize in exotic places and I mix and match what my clients want. Most of my customers are well off. A lot of them were former clients from my law practice days.

They don't want to be bothered with making the arrangements. They just tell me what they want, and I put it together."

The time passed so quickly. Jack looked at his watch. "I guess it's time to head home. I have a ton of paperwork to catch up on before I go back into the office. When will I see you again?"

"Probably Monday morning at work. I'll talk to Zeke about taking off for the holiday.

I think you've made me an offer I can't refuse."

He stood up and smiled down at her. "That's what I was hoping for." He grabbed her and kissed her again and she couldn't help herself, she kissed him back, hard and long.

He walked to the door, tilted his head and grinned.

"Until then." He waved as he left.

Gwen picked up Ethel, who was meowing loudly and began to pet her.

"I know, I know, but he is awfully nice, isn't he?"

12
ZEKE'S INVESTIGATION

Zeke kept batting zero. He had flashed Meg's picture around until the edges were worn and tattered. He checked out the bus station, the train depot, rental car agencies, Uber, airlines—not a sign of the missing girl anywhere. Her cell phone service had been cancelled.

He had better luck tracking her ex. After passing a few bucks around he did find out where Charlie was living and working. As of yet there were no parole violations, and Charlie was keeping up with his Anger Management Meetings. He was a star parolee. All Zeke could do was keep a tail on him. If Meg was hiding from him, Zeke knew she probably had good reason, presumably some kind of threat.

He talked to her close co-workers and casual friends. No one had a clue. If she were going to hide out far away, maybe there was a friend from the past who could help. He visited Mrs. Watkins again, grilling her about people Meg might contact. Zeke noted that his client looked thinner and a little paler than the last time he had seen her. The stress of having a missing daughter was beginning to show.

Clare led Zeke to her daughter's bedroom. Zeke noted that it still looked like a teenager's room. She reached into a trunk under the window and pulled out yearbooks and scrapbooks and laid them out on the fluffy pink covered bed. They sifted through the yearbooks and letters, cards and boxes of pictures.

"Who is this?" Zeke asked when he came across several pictures of the same girl.

"That's Carly. She and Meg were roommates all through their college years." Mrs. Watson looked at Zeke and he could feel the hope she held that this might be a lead. He did indeed think her old college roomie might be a possibility.

"Can you get in touch with her?" Zeke tried not to convey too much optimism.

Mrs. Watkins began bringing him up to date. "Carly married a young army doctor she met as a nurse in Afghanistan. A few years later he was killed in action. She's back in the states as far as I know. She lived with her family in New York for a while. I think she and Meg lost touch after that. She was such a darling girl. Very bright and energetic. Such a shame to have a tragedy in your life at such a young age."

"Do you have her family's address in New York by any chance?"

Clare began to feel hopeful. "No, but their name was Saunders. Her father was a doctor. An obstetrician, I believe. They live in Crystal Falls."

Zeke looked him up on his phone. "Here's his number. We don't want to say anything about Meg being missing. We just want to get Carly's address. You're going to call him and make something up. I know, say you're planning a surprise birthday party for Meg and you want to invite Carly. Ask for her address and phone number. Do you think you can handle it? You need to use your phone because he won't recognize my number."

Clare nodded yes and dialed. It was a little step in their search, but it made her feel like she was somehow helping Meg.

Zeke watched and listened as Clare spoke to Dr. Saunders. She spent five minutes talking about their daughters and remembering old times. Finally, she went into the pretext of planning a surprise birthday party for Meg and he gladly divulged Carly's address in Michigan.

There was no answer when they called the Michigan number, and a disappointed Mrs. Watkins left a message: "Carly, this is Meg's mother.

Could you call me back and let me know if you have heard from her, please?"

* * * * *

When Zeke came back to the office, Gwen was back from her continued surveillance of Meg's ex. She reported that everything was status quo.

Zeke nodded. "Well, I may have a lead on where she is. We left a message. Hopefully someone will call back." Zeke sat down at his desk and started to light up.

As if on cue, the phone rang. It was Mrs. Watkins. Zeke smashed his cigarette out in the over-flowing ashtray and answered.

"Carly returned my call. She said she hadn't heard from Meg. But I got the distinct feeling she was lying. Don't ask me why, I just have a mother's intuition." She started to cry.

"Don't worry now. As soon as I can get a chance I will take a little drive to Michigan and check it out. Don't worry, we'll find her." He hung up the phone and sighed, thinking of all of the cases he covered over the years that didn't turn out so well. He looked at Gwen.

"Well, I'm ready to close up for the day. What about you? Any loose ends?"

Gwen swallowed hard. "I'm wondering if I could take a few days off over Thanksgiving."

"That's possible. I'll probably close up the place for a few days. Nothing happens then anyway, and I am sure my Margie will have a boatload of errands for me to run. She invites all of our relatives who live in town over for Thanksgiving dinner. Are you going out of town?"

"Yeah, to Chicago… with Jack."

"Well, well, well," Zeke rubbed his hands together. "That's just great! That's just great. Have a wonderful time."

ANNETTE LACKNER

13
GINA

She parked her car in the lot at the starting point for the running trail, surprised to see only one other car. *I guess everyone is busy getting ready for the holiday weekend,* she thought. Gina got out and stretched to get ready for her run. *I need this more than ever with the holidays upon us,* she mused.

She smiled as she thought of her new husband, Mike, who was home preparing for Thanksgiving dinner, even though it was three days away. He loved to cook. Everyone they knew who was alone for Thanksgiving had been invited to join them on Thursday. Gina decided this would be a good time to go on her daily run and leave him in command of his culinary domain.

She jogged through the small, wooded arch that led to the trail. She entered and began to run slowly along the lake. It was a cool November morning, but the sun filtering through the autumn-colored leaves soon warmed her as she experienced the sense of freedom and control she so loved.

She hit her rhythm. Left foot, right foot, left foot, right foot. She felt the exhilaration kick in. Her mind was happy and clear. She pondered surviving an abusive marriage and how running in marathons had built her up physically as well as mentally. Yes, she was a strong woman now, stronger than ever. She approached the half-mile mark, keeping her stride. Left, right. Left, right. Her heightened senses heard a crunching noise off to the wooded side of the trail. *Probably a deer,* she thought. Left right. Left right.

She continued around the bend in the lake. A list of "to do's" was compiling in the back of her mind: how to arrange the tables, gather flowers from the garden and arrange them, pick up wine…. The crunch of leaves sounded again. She looked to her side, hoping to catch sight of a deer, but it was just a squirrel. Left, right. Left right.

The man in the forest made his way onto the running trail and stayed a good distance behind. Max knew he could easily catch up with her. He was in top form, even though he was no longer an agent. He worked out daily to maintain the fitness level needed for his line of work.

Gina slowed down a little as she approached the mile marker. She could do another mile or two easily. Left, right. Left right. The scattered trees shed a pattern of light that flickered bright then shadowy. Gina suddenly realized she was totally alone on the path.

Max accelerated his pace so that he was just a few feet behind her, a silk stocking in his hand.

The sound was on the trail behind her now. She pulled to the right of the path to make room for another runner, aware that a deer would never be that bold. Left, right. Left right. Gina turned around a little to see what was there. It wasn't an animal, it was another runner wearing a hoody and facemask.

Gina picked up the pace, hoping to outrun the threat, but she could hear his steps keeping up with her. Heart pounding, she was about to break into a sprint but he pounced before she could react to the force tightening around her neck. She flailed and tried to kick him where it would hurt the most. Left, right was still playing in her head as she gasped for one last breath.

He dragged her far into the woods where he stripped her naked. He was so aroused by her well-toned body he couldn't help fondling her breasts and the area between her legs where her sweet stuff was. As much as he wanted to penetrate her, he knew better than to leave his DNA. He was so aroused he removed his gloves, opened his fly and relieved himself into his own hand, thinking, *There has to be some kind of reward for this job that isn't just financial.*

He quickly stuffed his gloves into his backpack and made his way back to the trail, making sure he had left no evidence in the woods. He jogged nonchalantly back to the starting point, picked up the sign he had previously placed under the arch: "TRAIL CLOSED FOR MAINTENANCE." He tossed it into the trunk of the rental car then sped away.

There was a flight to Michigan waiting for him.

ANNETTE LACKNER

14
CHICAGO

The drive to Chicago was a pleasant one. They listened to music and sometimes sang along. Jack talked more about his son and his marriage. Gwen expressed her concerns about how Joe would feel about her being there with his father.

Jack laughed. "Are you kidding me? He's been after me for a long time to start dating. You see, he has finally moved on. He has a real sweet girlfriend, and he is almost 22. His life is in Chicago now. He hopes to get a job there when he graduates. I would be surprised if he doesn't ask Tracy to marry him. He seems nuts about her. But I know he worries about me. Nothing would make him happier than for his old man to move on with his own life."

Gwen chuckled as she took a sip from her coffee thermos. "It seems funny for someone to call you their old man."

Jack frowned. "Well, I'll take it from him," he glanced at Gwen, "but no one else." Traffic picked up as they got nearer to the big city.

The hotel was located right in the heart of downtown Chicago, close to the Magnificent Mile. The lobby was crowded with a swell of Thanksgiving travelers, but finally they took the elevator up to the 12th floor. Gwen was nervous. "It seems that you and I have an elevator thing going on," she joked.

They had two luxurious adjoining rooms with a spectacular view of the Windy City. Jack placed her bags on the bed and handed her the key card for her room.

"What if I make reservations here for dinner about seven and then we could walk around the city for a while. Does that sound okay? Meanwhile, I've got some business calls to make."

"I'd love it. It will give me a chance to relax and get freshened up for dinner."

Gwen turned the TV on and found a music station. She poured herself a soda from the complimentary bar and began to unpack. When she finished, she sat in the chair and sipped her drink, but unpleasant memories start creeping in. Immediately she got up and filled the tub, adding the bubble bath that sat in a complimentary container on the bathroom counter. She instantly relaxed as she eased her body into the soothing water. It wasn't long before memories of her second husband came wafting through the steamy cloud. She realized this hotel was probably the trigger. He wined and dined her in beautiful hotels such as this.

He slipped into her life when she was most vulnerable. Her parents paid her tuition to a beauty school, figuring she would be able to get a job right away and start paying her keep. She did get a job at a high-priced salon and worked her way up to a pretty good salary. Brandon had inherited an entire chain of salons from his parents. He came in about once a month to check the books and see how the business was running. He noticed Gwen right away. Gwen felt her good looks were an asset to her career and made the most of the makeup classes they provided, becoming a stylish, beautiful young woman. Eventually Brandon asked her out and soon they were seeing each other all of the time. She loved the glamour of going downtown to concerts, nice restaurants and the theater. He was well known around town, so it was an endless string of cocktail parties and dinner invitations. Thinking back, she realized now that it was security she had longed for. He was 20 years older and settled in life, divorced with grown children, so her inability to have a family wasn't a problem. She was desperate to get out of her parents' house. It was in hotels like this that he taught her how to please a man in bed and how to please herself.

They married within six months. It was the beautiful wedding she had always dreamed of, right from the cover of bridal magazines. Brandon rented an old estate that had been converted into an events venue. A florist provided the most beautiful flowers and decorations she could imagine. Gwen's parents were disappointed that she wasn't getting married in the church they attended, but since they didn't have to pay the wedding bills they relented. They lobbied for their church pastor to preside, but eventually agreed on a minister who came along with the package. Gwen didn't want anything affiliated with her childhood church to influence her wedding.

After a honeymoon in Paris, Brandon surprised her with a gorgeous home in one of the best neighborhoods and hired a professional to help her do the decorating. They traveled around the country and stayed at the best resorts. Gwen had everything a young woman could want: a beautiful home, a closet full of clothes, travel and security.

But she soon realized security had a price. She was the trinket on his arm. A pretty woman who showed the world he had everything a man could want. The first sign of trouble came at a dinner party. When she contradicted him on a major issue, he grabbed her wrist under the table and twisted it until she almost screamed with pain. She decided she wouldn't provoke Brandon that way again. When she came down in jeans to go out for a casual dinner, he took one look at her and yelled: "All the money I spend on clothes for you and you're wearing that?" She tried to hold her own, but he grabbed her arm and coldly said: "Go change." And she did, remembering the pain when she provoked her first husband, Mark.

She became all that he wanted her to be. She became nothing. She began feeling like a slave, even in the bedroom. After a few years, she even hated having sex with him. There was no foreplay. He stayed in his home office drinking vodka and tonic and talking on the phone, probably to other women, while she watched old movies in their den.

Then one night he started something new. He came into the den and said, "I am going up to bed are you coming?" This was his unoriginal signature line when he wanted to have sex.

"I'll be up as soon as this show is over." She was procrastinating. When she did go up to their room, she found a pair of red lace bikini underwear hanging on the doorknob. Instead of exciting her it made her feel sick. His lovemaking that night was almost violent. This game continued for a few years. The red panties meant kinky sex, the black meant normal sex and no panties meant no sex.

She went into his office one day to dust and vacuum and noticed he had left his computer on. She went over to investigate and found he was heavily into porn websites. Gwen realized, in horror, she was fulfilling his perverted fantasies.

Weeks later, when she went up to bed there were no panties on the doorknob. Gwen breathed a sigh of relief and went into the bathroom to wash her face and put on her nightgown. As she rinsed her face, suddenly Brandon was standing there naked. He grabbed her and pulled her roughly onto the bed. She saw a belt on each bedpost. "No, no, no," she whimpered. "No, Brandon."

"Come on, honey, it will be fun," he whispered as he tied each wrist to the bedposts then took her over and over. The more she screamed, the more excited he seemed to get. She quit screaming and just put up with it. It was that night when she understood what it was like to be raped.

Gwen realized she had to get away from him. She began sending little packages to her sister in Florida. Each parcel contained clothing, jewelry and some money, just enough that he wouldn't notice. Another year went by. It was a red panty night. He waited naked in the bed. He motioned for her to join him. She sat on the edge of the bed. He said, "I know I haven't been too nice to you lately, so I want to make it right." He handed her a leather switch and stretched across her lap. "Beat me. Beat me hard."

Gwen had visions of her father beating her mother; of Mark beating her in the little trailer. "Brandon, I can't do it. I'll do whatever you want but I can't beat you." She began to cry.

"Beat me, you bitch," he screamed, biting the flesh in her hip.

She beat him over and over with the switch. Suddenly she was hitting him harder and harder releasing all of her pent up anger while he came to a climax. When he was finally spent, she dropped the switch and ran to the bathroom to wash her face. When she looked into the mirror, she told her pathetic reflection this had to end. She had stayed too long. She waited until he was asleep and tiptoed downstairs to make her plans. She would fly to her sister's place and stay with her. There was the money she had sent, and she could sell the jewelry. Ali would help her find work. She fell asleep on the sofa in the den.

It was light when she awoke to the sounds of Brandon getting dressed for the day. Gwen made her way to the kitchen to brew the coffee. She would tell him today, she had to tell him today.

"Smells good." He crept up behind her and put his hand in her robe and began to fondle her breast. "Last night was great, babe."

She pulled away and closed her robe. Somewhere through that switch last night she found her courage. "Maybe for you, not for me. I'm finished, Brandon. I'm leaving you."

"Don't even think about it. You won't get a dime, nothing." He grabbed her by the wrist. "I can make your life hell, you ungrateful bitch."

"Let go of me."

He grabbed her by the hair and yanked her head back. "Never, I own you."

Suddenly she was in survival mode. She grabbed the coffee pot with her free hand and hit him in the face with it. Brandon stumbled back in shock and caught himself on the counter. He let go of her arm long enough to wipe his face with a dishtowel.

Gwen's rage continued. "Do you want me to call the police? Think of the scandal it would cause, that the perfect Brandon Prince was into porn and beating his wife!"

He glared at her through blood dripping from a cut over his eye. "Go get your things and get out of here. But remember, I will make your life hell. You won't have a penny to your name. Go on, get out," he screamed at her. He slapped her so hard she fell against the sink. "Get the hell out of my house. And don't think you can come crawling back. Other women are standing in line to take your place." He charged out to the garage, slamming the door.

Gwen pulled herself together and began picking up the pieces of the shattered coffeepot, wiped the brown liquid from the white tile floor, and placed it all in the trash can. She thought of her own broken life as she climbed the stairs to their bedroom. When she heard his car squeal down the street, she felt a certain calmness take hold and took a long shower, dressed and packed. She would spend the night in a hotel and make arrangements to go to Ali's place in Florida. She would put as much on her credit card as she could before he cancelled it. She was free. She was free.

The ringing phone jolted Gwen out of her past. She reached the wall phone from the sudsy tub to hear Jack's voice. "I'll be at your door in an hour, will you be ready?"

She instinctively tensed up for a second. "I'll be ready. I'm still in the tub. I lost track of time, but I'll be ready."

* * * * *

The hotel restaurant was elegant, enhanced by the piano music coming from the bar area. Jack pulled out her French provincial chair and smiled at her. "You look absolutely gorgeous."

She watched him sit down and realized she was falling in love for the first time in her life. It felt so different than it did with the other two men who came before. It felt so easy.

He looked into her eyes as the waiter poured the wine. "You look sort of sad tonight. Is everything okay?"

"This hotel brought back some bad memories of my second husband. He loved elegant hotels. When I left him and went to live with my sister Ali in Florida, I didn't care if I was ever in one again. And of course, he saw to it that I couldn't afford it if I wanted to. It's a long story, but he saw to it that I lost every job I found in Florida. That's what brought me back to Cincinnati. A friend offered me a job with her catering business and that's how I met Zeke. It was at cocktail party I catered. Long story short: here I am."

Jack grabbed her hands into his. "I'm so glad you are. Look, we don't have to eat here. We can take a walk down the Magnificent Mile and grab some burgers along the way. Let's get rid of those awful memories and make some of our own. There's nothing wrong with a good old hot dog or burger." He stood up, leaned his head a little and grinned. "Let's do it."

She stood up and took his hand in hers. "Okay, you're on."

They walked and gawked. They did grab a hot dog. Anything you would ever want was displayed in the windows along the way. She gazed through the window of FAO Schwarz and thought of the children she would never have.

"Anything a kid would want," Jack remarked.

"Everything but the most important thing."

"And what would that be?"

"Love. Just plain, ordinary love."

He smiled and kissed her. "Yes, but there is nothing ordinary about love." He kissed her again and laughed. "You taste like mustard."

"And you have pickle relish on the side of your mouth."

"Darn, and I was trying to be so suave. Ready to head back?"

"If you promise to buy me a banana split at that little ice cream parlor in the hotel. I've never had one before."

"Well, we'd better take care of that."

They looked like a pair of teenagers sitting on stools at the marble counter. The truth was, they felt like teenagers digging into the huge banana split with their own spoons. The couple talked and talked until the parlor turned off the Tiffany lamps and closed down for the night.

"Well, I guess it's time to head back to our rooms," Jack said as he led the way to the elevators. "At the elevators again."

As they entered the car and the doors closed, he pulled her into his arms and kissed her. "There. I've wanted to do that every time I saw you get on the elevator in the Arnold Building. My dream has come true."

When they got to her door, she kissed him goodnight, whispering, "I don't think I am ready yet."

"I can wait. I know you care for me. I've still got two more days to win you over. If you want to be won over."

"I do." She kissed him and unlocked her door. "Good Night. See you at breakfast."

15
MICHIGAN

Zeke decided to use the two days before Thanksgiving to take a little drive to Michigan. Margie had a fit about it. She wanted him to stay home and help. But then he started talking about the missing girl and her mother and he convinced his wife that he had to go. He first had to go to the liquor store and put the leaves in the dining room table, plus a few other errands before he left town.

He was pretty sure that he would find Meg living there with her former roommate, Carly. What worried him was that if it were this easy for him to find her it would also be easy for someone else.

The detective drove down the tree-lined neighborhood. The houses were turn-of-the-century architecture in various stages of renovation, and a slight trace of snow made it look like a scene on the front of a holiday card. He parked two doors away on the opposite side of the street and took time to study the missing girl's photo. Zeke reached over to the passenger side and grabbed an orange vest and a yellow hard hat and put them on along with a phony name badge and a clipboard.

He rang the bell and waited. Then he knocked loudly. He could see the door had a peep- hole and he knew someone was probably looking out. Then he saw her looking out the front window. It was definitely Meg, with short blond hair. *She is really scared if she changed her appearance*, Zeke thought. He knocked again calling, "Water man." After a few seconds he heard the knob turn and she answered the door and peered at him through the dead bolt chain. "Yes?"

"Sorry to disturb you, but we wanted to let you know we're going to be working on the water main. There's a chance your water will be off for a little while later on today. No need to call the water company, it won't be off too long. You'll have plenty of time to cook that Thanksgiving dinner. Hope it doesn't inconvenience you too much."

Zeke noticed her eyes darting up and down the street. Meg said, "Oh, I guess that guy a few doors down is with you then?" He sensed the relief in her voice, as she looked toward a tall blond man in a parka slowly meandering down the street.

"No, he's not one of our crew. Well, have a great turkey day. And I'm glad to see you take your safety seriously. You never know nowadays. Good afternoon." He tipped his yellow hard hat and smiled.

"Good-bye," she replied quickly closing the door. Zeke could hear the door lock click.

He returned to his car, grabbed his camera, and attached the zoom lens and snapped a few photos of the man down the street. "Come on, fella, turn toward me." Finally, the suspect crossed the street and started walking back. Zeke took a few more quick shots and drove away.

Well, at least he could tell Mrs. Watkins where her daughter was and that she was okay. It would give her hope, something to be thankful for on Thanksgiving Day. He began the long drive home to Cincinnati and Margie.

16

THANKSGIVING

They met at the luxurious buffet breakfast in the sunny, bustling hotel dining room.

Jack smiled and pulled out her chair. "The coffee is right here and good and hot, want some?"

She nodded "yes" and held out her cup. "I really need it. I didn't sleep that well last night." She could feel herself blush.

He looked her square in the eyes. "Neither did I." He lowered his eyes. "So, what are you going to do today while I'm working? Can I call a taxi for you or something?"

"I think I'll be okay. I'll just freelance. I know that you and Zeke think I'm nuts, but I want to check into the murder of that girl here in Chicago. The one I told you about who was killed right after my friend Julia died. I just feel it in my bones that they're connected in some way. They both attended support groups. They both were starting over. Something just doesn't feel right about it. How do I begin?"

"Probably read everything you can find in the newspapers about the murder. You can do that right here in the hotel on the computer. Just go to the *Chicago Tribune*'s website. I know Julia's sister doesn't think her death was an accident but that's a common thing with grieving people. After all, her husband was Judge Kildeer. How could he be involved?"

Gwen hesitated and took a deep breath before she spoke. "Jack, I'm not supposed to discuss anything divulged in our meetings, but I know I can trust you. The honorable Judge Kildeer abused Julia horribly.

I know she asked for the divorce and got a settlement. Why wasn't it in the papers? Why wasn't it a big scandal?"

"Judge Kildeer an abuser! Wow, that's so hard to believe." Jack took a sip of his coffee and mulled over her question for a minute. "Well, it could mean that they settled out of court. And, knowing who he is, that would be most advantageous to him, and a large settlement would allow her to go on with her life."

"And that could be a motive for murder! Money or revenge," Gwen said loud enough to make the couple at the adjacent table turn their heads in their direction. Gwen chomped down on the crispy piece of her toast in her hand and lowered her voice. "Let's eat. I have a lot to do today."

Jack let out a deep sigh. "Why don't you do something fun, like shopping or sightseeing?"

"I'll probably do a little of that, too," she said, thinking to herself that she would do what she damn well pleased.

After they ate a huge breakfast and kissed good-bye, Gwen made a dash for the business office and parked herself at one of the computer modules.

She read every article about the murder, taking notes along the way. The first time she looked down at her watch it was 1:00 p.m. *No wonder my stomach is growling*, she mused. She picked up her notes and went to the hotel coffee shop and ordered a sandwich. The only solid information was that Maura had moved to Chicago from Cincinnati and frequented the Bee Hive Bar, where she was seen for several nights with the same man. There were no clues in her apartment. Her ex-husband, a long-distance trucker, was a suspect for a while because she had sued him for assault and battery. But after checking it out, police found he had a rock-solid alibi. Gwen wasn't surprised about the abuse. After all, the victim, Maura Di Angelo, did belong to a support group.

She went out through the bustling hotel entrance and had the doorman hail her a taxi. When Gwen told the tired looking driver she wanted to go to the Bee Hive Bar and Grill, he gave her a strange look. "You sure, Miss? That's a pretty rough part of town. There was even a murder there not too long ago."

"I know. I'm doing an investigation for a detective in Cincinnati. I will want you to wait at the curb for me and bring me back to the hotel. Is that okay?"

The cabbie shrugged his shoulders. "Sure, it's your money."

About 20 minutes later they pulled up in front of a neon sign that depicted a beehive with little flashing bees buzzing around it. It looked pretty shady, but Gwen confidently marched through the door, past a few squirrely looking men sitting on bar stools. She looked around and found a waitress taking an order. Gwen approached her with her ID from Zeke's. "I wonder if I could ask you a few questions about Maura Di Angelo?"

The silver-haired waitress looked her up and down. "I've told the cops everything I know." Gwen touched the woman's shoulder as she started to turn away.

"Well, I actually work for a private detective in Cincinnati. We're just going over everything one more time. Tell me what you remember about Maura."

The waitress stuck her order tablet into the pocket of her uniform apron and gave Gwen an exasperated glare. "She was sexy. Flaunted it, if you know what I mean. Lookin' for love in all the wrong places, if you know what I mean. She'd let any guy in the place buy her drinks. Then a week before her murder, she was here every night with the same guy. Probably, he's the one who killed her."

"What did he look like?"

The woman shrugged her shoulders. "Big guy, reddish brown hair pulled back in a ponytail at the base of his neck."

The bartender hollered, "Maggie, we got customers here."

"Okay, okay." Maggie made a face. "I gotta get back to work."

"Just one more thing. Did you ever talk to her?"

Maggie paused. "Yeah, one night in the ladies room. She was putting on her bright red lipstick. I told her: 'Be careful, there's some real monsters out there.' She said to me and I quote: 'Don't worry about me, I was married to one for twelve years. I know how to handle monsters.' Maggie shrugged again. "Well, I guess she didn't, did she?"

"Maggie!" Another shout from behind the bar.

"I really gotta get back to work," Maggie said as she walked away.

Gwen looked around for the restroom. She stepped inside and just stood there remembering the conversation the waitress relayed to her. She could almost feel Maura's presence asking Gwen to find the monster who had murdered her.

Gwen ran out to the waiting taxi and went straight back to the hotel, where she immediately took a hot shower.

After she dressed, she sat in the over-stuffed chair and put up her feet, deciding to read the *Cincinnati Enquirer* online. "Oh, my God!" she whispered into the empty air. A young woman had been found dead near a local jogging trail, apparently strangled. There was a grainy picture of a wooded area surrounded with yellow tape and police looking for evidence. Just next to that picture was a picture of the victim. Police were still investigating.

* * * * *

They ordered a light dinner in the hotel dining room, saving their appetite for Thanksgiving dinner tomorrow. Gwen shared her findings with Jack and told him about the girl who was strangled in Cincinnati. "There's something in common with Julia and Maura. They were both married to monsters. They were both starting over. I did some computer research on Gina, the strangled woman. She was married before. I did some research on her ex. He spent time in jail.

I couldn't find anything on abuse, but I wouldn't be surprised. Then, I checked in with Zeke today. He has located the missing girl we've been looking for. She's okay, but there is someone stalking her. I've been tailing her ex and he was an abuser. Jack, I just know that there is some connection between all of these murders!"

Jack looked at her over his wine glass as he took a sip. When he spoke to her his voice had an edge to it. "Gwen, have you considered the idea that maybe you are seeing that connection because you were so abused. It's bringing back all that you've been through. After all, these women died in three different states. Just put it aside for a while and relax. How about it?"

"I am long past any man telling me what I should or should not do," she snapped.

"Not every male in the world is a monster. I hope you realize that by now." There was a tone of anger in his voice.

He's right, she thought. *And now I have hurt him. He's been so patient with me. What am I doing? Am I purposely trying to throw this whole relationship away?* She collected herself and said: "Maybe you're right. And no, not every man in this world is a monster, especially the one sitting here. I am sorry, Jack. You know I am still trying to work through things. I am so sorry." She took his hand and put it against her cheek. "Apology accepted?"

"Of course. Let's finish eating and go into the bar. The music sounds great. Let's dance the night away and forget about all of this gruesome stuff."

They ordered after-dinner drinks in the bar and slow danced to the blues. He held her tight around the waist as she laid her head against his chest. Gwen looked up at him. "I needed to be held tonight."

He kissed the top of her head and pressed against her. "So did I, Gwen, so did I."

They didn't leave the dance floor until the music stopped.

They held hands on the elevator in silence. When they reached Gwen's door Jack kissed her. It was a good-night kiss. He looked her in the eyes. "Let's start over tomorrow and make it just about you and me. I've had a lot of memories of Kay tonight. I guess I'm not as ready as I thought I was."

Gwen smiled and put her hand on his arm. "You're right. Let's start over again tomorrow. Just you and me, no ghosts." She kissed him and went through the door.

Gwen was crying as she undressed. As soon as she was in her pajamas, she did what she always did at a time like this. She called her sister Ali.

"Hi, Gwen? It's eleven o'clock? What's up?" She could hear the concern in Ali's voice.

She filled Ali in on the murders and her interest in them. Then she went into the weekend here with Jack and how she spoiled their evening together.

"Look, Jack's right. Just start over tomorrow. It sounds like you really have fallen for this guy. He sounds wonderful. And you know you wouldn't have come with him if you weren't interested in having a relationship with him."

Gwen wiped her tears with the palm of her hand. "I think I'm falling in love with him. I really want to sleep with him, but now I think I've ruined everything."

"Just see how tomorrow plays out. If you want to sleep with him do it. It doesn't mean you have to marry him. Just let go and enjoy Thanksgiving with him. Now go to bed and get a good night's sleep. I love you, Sis."

"Same here. I'll call you tomorrow night." Gwen turned out the light, fearing the nightmares that had haunted her for years.

* * * * *

Joe had made dinner reservations at a new restaurant near the university, which was featuring a traditional Thanksgiving dinner served family style. It was an old Victorian house decorated in furniture from the same period. It had a warm, homey feeling, almost as good as being in a real home surrounded by extended family. Joe and his girlfriend were waiting at the table for them. It was a little awkward at first, but soon their conversation became easy and cordial. Gwen was happy to see that Joe possessed the same easy-going personality as his father.

Jack picked out a white wine and poured. Between bites of shrimp cocktail, Gwen asked Tracy about her studies. Tracy was from Illinois and was studying to be a teacher. Joe talked about the engineering school and his plans to stay there after graduation, possibly working toward his masters. They were obviously in love. Gwen pushed back her own feelings of inadequacy, reminding herself that a degree doesn't always make you successful in life. After all, she once had a successful career in a prestigious salon making really good money. That is, until she married the wrong guy.

Their server arrived with a cart filled with a platter of steaming turkey, dressing that filled the air with the aroma of sage and onion, a beautiful casserole of mixed roasted vegetables, and an assortment of potatoes: mashed, sweet and oven roasted. As they enjoyed their dinner, Gwen realized she had never cooked a Thanksgiving dinner before and wondered if Kay was a good cook.

"What kind of pie?" Jack was staring at her. "You're a million miles away."

Gwen laughed. "It must be a food coma setting in." She looked up at a waiter standing beside a cart with a variety of pies and a pumpkin roll. "I'll have pumpkin pie, the one with the most whipped cream."

"Me, too. We can walk it off later." Jack smiled at her as Tracy and Joe exchanged a knowing look.

Over coffee and dessert, Joe and Jack discussed plans for the Christmas holidays. The young couple wanted to visit with Tracy's family for a few days and then drive down to Cincinnati to spend the rest of the time with Jack.

Jacks said, "That's great. Even if I don't get you for Christmas, we can ring in the New Year together."

Joe's words came stumbling out. "That is, if you don't already have plans." He glanced at Gwen. "I shouldn't assume you're free, Dad."

Jack put his arm casually around Gwen's shoulder. "We'll make sure we are free, right Gwen?"

She felt herself tingle inside. Jack had said "we." She nodded, "Of course, we'll be free."

Tracy and Gwen stood under the restaurant awning while Joe and Jack went through the drizzling rain to get the cars.

"Gwen, I just want you to know that Joe is really happy about his dad seeing someone seriously. He worries so much about him being alone. He says he hasn't heard his dad sound so optimistic in a long time. And I can't speak for Joe, but I like you very much."

Gwen felt tears well up and suddenly realized how much it meant to her to be accepted by these two young people. She knew she was no longer falling in love with Jack. She *was* in love with Jack.

* * * * *

They were quiet on the ride back to the hotel, both feeling the need for each other welling up and almost spilling over.

The doorman opened the door for them as Jack took her hand. "How about a few times around the dance floor before we turn in."

They danced holding on to each other as if they were afraid something would pull them apart. *No ghosts*, Gwen told herself. She felt warm and secure as they swayed back and forth, no longer really dancing, just holding each other like something they had lost had been found again. They danced until the last song.

"Let's go upstairs," Jack whispered into her ear.

"Let's," she whispered back. They rode up in the elevator staring into each other's eyes knowing that the time was finally here. She put the card in the slot and opened the door and motioned for him to enter.

He closed the door and gazed at her. "I think maybe I'll have a lot to be thankful for this Thanksgiving." He gently kissed her and ran his fingers through her hair and down her neck to her breasts. She pulled away and let her dress drop to the floor, then removed her underwear. She took him by the hands and pulled him toward her bed. Then she helped him undress. Their lovemaking was tender, each wanting to please the other rather than themselves. When he entered her, she knew this was the way it should be; this is what it felt like to be truly loved. His thrusts were gentle until they both reached a climax at the same time. He laid on top of her for a long time, kissing her face and ears.

Jack rolled to his side and pulled her to him spoon style. "Gwen, I love you. I want to be with you."

"I feel the same," she murmured. They fell asleep in each other's arms.

When Gwen awoke a few hours later, Jack was awake, lying on his back and staring up at the ceiling. She kissed his shoulder. "Didn't you sleep?"

"Like a baby for a few hours. I was afraid I wouldn't please you. It's been quite a while. I'm afraid I'm out of practice."

"Oh, you pleased me. You know what they say." She climbed on top of him. "Practice makes perfect."

This time their lovemaking was urgent. They allowed the built-up sexual tension between them to take over. It was as desperate as the first time had been gentle. When it was over, they were exhausted, physically and mentally. They fell into a deep sleep, never leaving each other's arms.

When Gwen woke up again she saw a slit of sunlight coming through the drapes. Then her eyes saw Jack sitting in the chair in sweatpants and a tee shirt, staring at her. She stretched her arms into the air. "What time is it?"

"Its 10:45. I've been watching you sleep, telling myself how lucky I am that you bumped into me that day. You know, I felt it then, that you might be the one." He paused, then stood. "Are you hungry?"

She sat up and pulled up the sheet to cover her breasts. "I could eat a horse. But first, coffee."

"Your wish is my command." He went over to the table and poured two cups from a fresh pot. "I had them deliver it to my room a little while ago. I went over and took a shower and dressed. What do you like in it?"

"Straight, please."

"How about room service for breakfast?"

"You read my mind." She jumped out of bed and ran to the bathroom, returning in the hotel's monogrammed robe.

"You look very sexy in your bare feet with your hair all messed up," he said.

She came over and kissed him gently. "Let's have breakfast first."

Gwen went in and took a shower and freshened up. She heard the breakfast being delivered and then came out to see a table set up with linens and flowers. Delicious aromas were escaping from under the silver lids. Jack pulled out a chair for her and then seated himself. They both ate like the Thanksgiving feast never happened: eggs, bacon, fruit and pastries.

"I was thinking," Jack said, sipping on his coffee. "I don't have to be back until Monday. How about you?"

"Nope," she mumbled through pastry in her mouth.

"What if we stay today and tomorrow and drive back on Sunday."

"That sounds perfectly wonderful. I just have to call my neighbor to keep taking care of Ethel."

"Oh, Ethel. That's right. I forgot about her. She'll really hate me now, for keeping you away longer."

Gwen went over and sat on his lap. "Let's not worry about Ethel right now."

She went over and crawled into bed and patted the pillow next to her. Jack put the breakfast cart out in the hall and placed the "Do Not Disturb" sign on the door. He grinned. "I think it's time for more practice."

They made love and slept and talked and made love and slept again. Jack confided everything about his life and Gwen everything about hers. She kissed his tears away when he talked about losing Kay and he wiped hers away when she talked about losing her baby. He kissed the tiny scar from the Caesarian section. "I love you, Gwen, I've known it from the first time I saw you."

"Oh, Jack, I love you too. I was just so afraid of being hurt again. How could I have ever thought that you could be like the others?"

"Gwen, you keep wondering why you picked two abusers, but think about it. You didn't really pick them. Your parents forced you into your first marriage. When you married the second one, you were looking for security. I don't think you really loved either one of them. I want you to be in love with me for who I am, warts and all. I want to share my life with you."

Gwen pulled him close. "I do want to share your life and all that comes with it. But for now, how about sharing a nice dinner from room service? We can always sightsee tomorrow."

ANNETTE LACKNER

17
BACK TO WORK

When Zeke returned from Michigan he found Margie, up to her elbows in food. She was chopping and dicing vegetables for tomorrow's dinner. The pies were sitting on a metal rack on top of the counter. She had been very busy while he was gone. Even though their Thanksgiving guests would bring dishes with them, it was a lot of work for Margie to do alone. He immediately felt guilty, and although he was bone tired, he pitched right in to help get things ready for tomorrow's feast.

The dinner they shared with Margie's sister and her daughter and Zeke's brother and his family was delicious. Their families were close, and they shared stories of past Thanksgivings, over-ate, watched a little football and then did Zoom time with their absent family members. More than anything else, they were thankful for each other's love. Zeke thought about Mrs. Watkins and silently prayed she would have Meg back with her next year.

Before he went to the office on Monday, Zeke stopped by and had a friend develop the pictures of the stranger from Michigan. He felt so good when he told Mrs. Watkins that Meg was living with Carly in Michigan and that he personally talked to her. He then stopped by her house to show her the picture of the stranger on the street. Mrs. Watkins had no idea of who it might be. They went through all of Meg's old pictures and yearbooks, but found no matches.

When he finally got to the office, he was surprised that Gwen was late. She had never been late before. He spread the newspaper out on his desk, opened the window a little and lit up a cigarette. He began reading about the funeral of the young woman who was strangled a few days before Thanksgiving. Police were warning women not to go jogging alone and to be aware of their surroundings no matter how safe they felt.

"Well, well, the usual cloud of smoke rising from the paper." Gwen went over and closed the window. She wrapped her arms around herself and gave a shivering motion. "Don't you know it's cold out there?"

Zeke glanced up from the paper. "'Well, well, well' yourself. You're late, young woman.

What's your excuse?"

Gwen smiled. "Jack and I stayed over an extra day in Chicago. We didn't get in until late last night."

"Is that right. You must have had a great time." He flashed a knowing grin.

"Zeke, you're the only one I am telling this, but Jack and I are… I guess you could say… an item. He asked me to marry him over New Years while his son is in town, but I don't think I'm ready for another marriage."

Zeke came from behind his desk and gave her a huge bear hug. "That's great news. I was hoping this would develop. I'm a sucker for a good love story."

"You think I don't know that? You'll be the first one to know if I say yes." She put her bag down and pulled a chair up to his desk. "So, fill me in on what's happening." He told her about his trip to Michigan and showed her the picture of the stranger. Gwen glanced down at the newspaper lying on Zeke's desk. "What's new on the girl who was strangled?"

"Nothing much. No leads as yet. I did some nosing around on Saturday and found out her ex-husband was questioned, but he had a solid alibi. He spent some time in jail for roughing her up during an argument."

"I suspected as much. I did some research and saw that he had a record."

"You're becoming quite the detective. I thought you were in Chicago for a weekend getaway," Zeke teased.

Gwen ignored his comment. "There's more. I checked out the bar where the murdered girl from Cincinnati was last seen. She told the waitress that she was married to a monster for twelve years. Zeke, I just know these murders are all connected somehow. Call it woman's intuition or whatever you want. Julia, Maura, this strangled woman and Meg were all married to abusers. Two of them went to 'help' groups. Meg was probably threatened by her ex and that's why she's in hiding."

Zeke scribbled doodles on the note pad in front of him. "Well, I am open to the possibility now, but all of their exes have rock solid alibis. We'll keep checking this out, but in the meantime we have to make sure that Meg stays safe where she is. I want you to keep up the tail on her ex today. Maybe follow him after work."

"I'm on it." She was beginning to like this job.

ANNETTE LACKNER

18
SURVEILLANCE

Gwen had been tailing Charlie for several days. Zeke wanted her to do a Saturday and see if anything new might develop. She parked a few doors from his apartment and waited. She called Jack several times to pass the hours. They had plans for dinner tonight at his place. He was cooking. She couldn't wait to be with him in his own surroundings.

Jack was describing the dinner he had planned when she noticed a black pick-up truck pull up in front of Charlie's apartment. The driver got out and locked the car. There was something so familiar about him; his build, the way he walked… "Oh my God," was all she could say over and over. She blinked her eyes a few times, to make sure she wasn't seeing things. There, in front of her, was her first husband, the monster who killed her baby, all decked out in Camo. She watched him enter the apartment building still trying to convince herself it was the beast who almost destroyed her.

"Jack, I have to go. Something's happening."

"I don't like the sound of this. Please be careful." She could hear the worry in his voice.

"Don't worry, I'll call you back as soon as I can."

Gwen kept her eyes glued on the apartment entrance. About 20 minutes later, Mark came out with Charlie by his side. Charlie was also dressed in hunting clothes.

She immediately called Zeke. "You won't believe this, but Charlie was just picked up by my first husband. It's looks like they're going hunting or something. The scary thing is that Mark wouldn't recognize a deer unless it was in his headlights. I'm going to follow them." Gwen threw her car into gear and took off.

"Okay, just be careful. Don't take any chances. I can track you from my cell. Keep in contact with me so I know that you are all right."

"Will do. We're heading north on I-75. This is too creepy, tailing my first husband. What are the odds?"

Then, it occurred to her that she was following a pair of abusers to God knows where.

19
THE JUDGE

He placed the final log on the fire and poured himself a scotch. His associates would arrive at the cabin in about an hour, just before dark. He arranged the large room just like he arranged his courtroom. He was a stickler for order. His life had been in order from the first breath he took. He came from a long line of judges, senators and congressmen. He was educated and groomed to follow in their footsteps. Every Sunday morning he arrived at church exactly 15 minutes before the service began, taking his rightful place in his family's pew. He never questioned his entitlement, his advantages; he did what was expected, knowing it would pay off in the end. Perhaps someday he would be a United States senator and enjoy the respect and benefits that came with the position.

He glanced down at the list of names: Julia, Maura, Gina—done. He took great pride in the fact that his plan was going exactly as designed. There were nine left. He sat back in the overstuffed easy chair and closed his eyes, enjoying the scent of the burning wood. His mind went to his courtroom, where he had first met the men who would be joining him soon; all found guilty of abuse. He had presided over so many of these cases where the law always favored the women who filed suit. He remembered the case that led him down this path so many years ago.

Mark was just a kid, his whole life ahead of him. But, like so many others, a bitch that pressed charges destroyed his life. It's hard to get a job with that kind of record. The women didn't mind screwing them and pushing them into a marriage they didn't want, but then goaded them to the point where they became abusive. As far as the judge was concerned, the wives got what they deserved and better. He seethed at the fact that these men had to attend "anger management" classes. That anger could have been managed by getting rid of their wives.

He decided as a judge, he would sit in on some of the classes that the law forced these men to attend. He went and listened. He didn't think these classes would change a thing. The attendees were there because they were ordered to be there. But the judge learned more than he expected. Mark talked about how he couldn't find work. He learned carpentry while in prison and became quite good at the trade. However, with his prison record he couldn't find a decent job.

It occurred to the judge that he finally could do something to help these men, since the law wouldn't. He started hiring them. Mark was first. He gave him a job rebuilding his screened-in porch and kept him on as a handyman. He engaged Maura's husband, Ralph, as his driver, because of his experience as a truck driver. He gave the other husbands work in their fields, recommending them to his vast circle of friends. He let them know, little by little, that he was simpatico with their anger, but had to follow the law, no matter how biased it was in favor of women.

It was Julia, his own wife, who pushed him over the edge. He had given her everything—a beautiful home in the best neighborhood and the best schools for their daughter. That bitch lacked for nothing. A country club membership, golf lessons, garden club, bridge groups— she was on the symphony board, for Christ sakes! She rode on the wave of his name and family's prestige. But just like his mother, she was never satisfied. It was always something: You're not home enough; I don't want to go to the charity event; I don't care for the Thompsons; let's go somewhere else for dinner tonight.... It never let up. Most of the time he just tuned her out. He did, though, insist on order and neatness in his home. Julia knew he couldn't stand dishes in the sink, newspapers laying on the sofa, or clothes on the floor, and he realized that sometimes she did those things just to irritate him. Those were the things that threw him into a rage. He handled Julia the way his father handled his mother. You have to smack them into shape every once in a while. That tactic did work for a while, but then Julia started drinking and threatening to tell people that he abused her. That's when he locked her in the walk-in bedroom closet for a few days. She was quiet as a mouse after that little punishment. But then after a few months she told him she wanted a divorce. That's when he lost it. He beat her until she was a whimpering blob in the corner of their bedroom, then locked the door and left in a rage.

It was several months later that he was approached by a friend at the club who was the top divorce lawyer in town. The lawyer asked him to join him for a drink in The Grill Room for some business. The judge sat beside him and talked sports and other small talk until their drinks arrived. Then the lawyer passed him a manila envelope. The judge's antennae went up. What was this, a bribe of some kind? He pulled out the contents to see large glossy photos of Julia's face staring back at him through black eyes and a bruised, swollen face. He froze for a moment, then quickly pushed them back into the envelope, looking around the room to make sure no one else had come in.

"You don't need to say a thing," his drinking companion said. "Here's the deal. We've discussed all of her options. She won't take it public for the sake of your daughter and your career. For the sum of three million dollars and a guarantee that you will continue to support your daughter's education, she will settle out of court. People aren't stupid, David. How many times can someone fall down the steps or be in a fender-bender? They will start putting two and two together."

The Judge threw the envelope back at him. "Three million! That's downright vicious," he snarled.

The lawyer grabbed him by the collar and pushed the envelope in his face. "So is this! Take it or leave it. It's your career, you piece of shit."

And that was that. Soon his marriage was over, and he was out $3 million. Julia had gotten the best of him. That thought festered in him like a cancerous tumor. It kept growing and growing. He would lie awake at night figuring out ways to kill her without getting caught. He wanted to kill all of the whining, pathetic women who testified in his courtroom. One sleepless night he put on the movie channel that showed oldies. He was watching Hitchcock's *Strangers on a Train* when it came to him: Have someone else do it. That was his answer. Do a switch, perhaps, with some of the men he had mentored over the years.

From that point on, he felt them out. He knew Mark would be the most open to it. Mark was building some shelves in the garage for him one afternoon, when the judge asked him to sit down on the patio and have a beer with him. Mark looked out at the perfectly manicured grounds of the estate, thinking that some people have all the luck. But he realized it wasn't luck at all, it was to whom and where you were born. The judge filled the carpenter in on what Julia had done to him.

"Whew, three million! I didn't know there was that much money in the world. No wonder you're pissed. I would kill for that much money!" He put the can of beer to his mouth and had a swig, remembering the bruises and black eyes he had seen on Julia.

"Would you?" Judge Kildeer paused, and then went on. "Would you kill your ex-wife if you had that much money?"

"I would pay someone else to do it, so I don't go to jail. I already did time for beating her up." Mark laughed and stood up. "I guess I'd better get back to work."

"No, no, have another beer. I have a little plan I want to discuss with you." He reached into the built-in cooler and pulled out another cold one which he passed to Mark. "I'd like to kill my ex-wife and you would like to kill your ex-wife for destroying your life. Am I correct?"

Mark hesitated, unsure of where this random conversation was leading. "Yeah, I could have had a football scholarship and made it to the pros if it wasn't for her messing up my life. What's your plan?"

"You know I have mentored several young men like you over the years, don't you?"

Mark nodded in affirmation. He had run into many of them here on the judge's property.

"In fact, the number comes to eleven men who have been screwed by their wives, twelve including me. Do you know what the irony of that is?"

Mark was cautious. "No, sir."

"It's the number of a jury; a jury of one's peers. A jury that can condemn the offenders."

"But we couldn't take it to court, could we?" Mark was thinking maybe the judge knew a way they could do it.

"No, no, Mark. We are a court of our own. I thought about having us kill each other's wives. However, that would be too risky. Too much room for errors and we want no errors. So, we form a group and hire a hit man. I have connections. I'm sure I can come up with one."

Mark sipped on his beer to stall for time and think through what was coming his way. "Are you really serious, or is there more than beer in that can?" He tried to read the judge's face. "If this is some kind of set-up, I'm out of here."

Kildeer smiled and spoke in a fatherly voice. "Mark, I think you know me better than that by now. Why do you think I hired you and the others? I feel that the law failed you. I want to help you get your pound of flesh and punish the one responsible. I promise you this is · not a 'set up,' as you called it. I want my wife eliminated and you feel the same way about yours."

"But even if we all agree, the rest of us don't have enough dough to do that." Mark was starting to trust his mentor's intentions.

"It wouldn't be needed. You will be doing me a favor. You supply the information to the hit man about your ex-wives. Where they eat, their hobbies, their time schedules and so forth. In return, I will continue to throw work your way, and as soon as I can work out a way to do it, I will have your records wiped clean. The plan is flawless. You won't need an alibi because you won't know when it's going to happen. You'll have no connection to it at all. We will all be beholden to each other since we are all in on it."

"So, you think you could have my record erased?"

The judge put on his most somber face as he lied. "I am sure of it. I just have to be discrete about it. It could take a little while, especially since I have to do it eleven times."

"Can I have time to think about it?" Mark watched a cardinal fly up to the birdbath, and then roost on the edge of the bowl.

"Sure, sure. Just think about the satisfaction of getting back at your ex. It's a perfect plan."

20

MEETING

The judge knew his greatest challenge was to secure a hit man. He spent weeks going through old court records, staying up late into the night, trying to come up with someone; someone who lurked in the background in one of the many ghastly cases that were tried in his courtroom. But he kept coming up dry. When it happened, it was quite by chance. It was at his monthly luncheon with his father at the country club, a practice they began when his father retired.

His father, the one-time senator, was still very active. He served on several boards and helped his political party by doing fundraisers when needed. He approached their pre-arranged table in the Grill Room, suntanned and healthy looking, sporting his golf attire. It was one of those beautiful Indian summer days when die-hard golfers took to the course one last time before the really bad weather set in. "I'll have a martini," he told the approaching waiter as he sat down. He looked at the judge and smiled. "How are you, Son?"

"I'm doing okay. It's been hard to get used to being a bachelor again, but I'm adjusting."

He sipped on his iced tea and motioned to their waiter that they were ready to order. "Do you want your usual, Dad?"

"Sure, that's fine."

The bow-tied waiter took their order and vanished into the kitchen area.

The senator sipped on his martini and waved back to a table of fellow members, then turned his attention to his son. "Well, keeping busy helps. You know you're probably better off. Once someone starts drinking the way Julia did it just goes from bad to worse. How is Krista doing?"

"I think she is okay. She loves college. I think she may go into law like the rest of us."

The senator grinned from ear to ear. "Well, well, that's fantastic. Tell her she can call on her old granddad for advice at any time."

Their food appeared quickly because the staff was aware of how important it was to serve the judge and his father promptly. The judge wanted to be in and out in exactly one hour, no "ifs" "ands" or "buts."

"Oh, by the way, I ran into an old friend of yours last week. Remember Max Chaney, your old fraternity brother?"

"Where on earth did you run into him? I heard he was a top agent in the CIA." The judge glanced at his watch to keep track of the time.

His father lowered his voice. "Not anymore. I went to Arkansas last week for an emergency board meeting of OCTOPUS, the private military complex. You know I sit on the board of directors. I ran into him on a tour of the facility. He asked me to give you his regards. He's one of their most prized people in the field. Turns out he was demoted in the CIA because of getting involved in some alleged torture or something. OCTOPUS snatched him up in a flash. He's considered a real killer, someone they can count on to deliver the goods in covert war activities."

"Well, what do you know? I always considered him a bit of a Boy Scout. Why was there an emergency meeting, Dad?"

The senator swallowed a bite of his sandwich and wiped his mouth with his napkin. "It seems they might have to shut down and regroup again under another name. The scuttlebutt is that Max and his crew set off a bomb somewhere and a lot of civilians were killed. That's why he's back in the country. The Afghanis want us out, or they go public with our whole enterprise, which won't sit well with the American voters. We're trying to forestall but it's not looking good. If we have to, we'll shut down and after a cooling off period we'll open again under another name."

While they finished lunch over small talk, the son's brain was in over-drive. Max could be the one, the final step in his plan.

They were presented with the bill to sign in precisely one hour and the two men parted ways.

The judge's whole being was filled with excitement as he walked down the hallway flanked with pictures of the club's founders, one of which was his own grandfather.

Back in his chambers, he spent some time thinking about Max Chaney. The term "real killer" hung in the back of his mind like a post-it note. Max was very popular with his friends. He was always there to help others when needed. He took part in every good cause. But, when he thought on a deeper level, he remembered Max during their hazing of pledges. He was the one who always held someone's head under water a little longer than everyone else. So long that it made the others a little uncomfortable. "Come on, man, enough," someone would holler, and he would stop. Max's practical jokes always went a bit too far. He remembered a Halloween Party. Their house-mother stayed a little late to set things up. She was alone in the kitchen rinsing off dishes and turned around to see a masked monster holding a knife. Poor old thing, she screamed and fainted. The others ran into the kitchen to see her on the floor; Max just stood there with a smile on his face. Only after others bent down to help her up did he apologize and get her some water.

The judge decided to keep Max on his short list of possibilities. He started laying the groundwork. He made a call to his father asking if he could get Max's contact information. He'd like to get in touch with his old friend just to get caught up. His father called back a few days later with the address and phone number. Max was living in a condo in Little Rock, waiting out the shutdown. When he got him on the phone, Max sounded genuinely pleased to hear from him and recalled running into the judge's father.

"I have to come to Little Rock to meet with a couple of lawyers about a case," the judge said. "I thought maybe we could get together for dinner while I'm there." He gave Max the dates he had cleared on his calendar and they agreed to meet for dinner at his hotel near the airport. He smiled as he put down his phone. One more step forward in his plan.

* * * * *

Kildeer placed his single bag in the luggage compartment and sat down in his first-class seat. He would have to change planes in Atlanta. As he fastened his seatbelt, a lovely young flight attendant approached. "Can I get you a drink, sir?"

"That would be great. How about your best scotch on the rocks?"

She smiled. "Anything else?" She glanced at the seat next to him. "I see you have your pillow and blanket. If you need anything else, let me know." She walked back to her station and pulled the privacy curtain.

There was something about her; her soft, calm tone of voice, or maybe the way her silky dark hair was styled, the grace in her walk. She reminded him of Julia. Julia when he married her, long before their marriage went south and her love affair with the bottle started.

One of his fraternity friends had invited Julia and a group of her friends to one of their keg parties. He was instantly attracted to her quiet beauty and struck up a conversation. She was attending the college of nursing and the judge was studying to get into law school.

They began seeing each other regularly. They were both huge University of Cincinnati football fans and went to all of the games together. The couple attended many of the social activities that the campus and the city of Cincinnati provided.

Julia's parents had divorced when she was in the fourth grade. She told him how her father just walked away and never came back. Her mother had a good job in marketing and traveled constantly; they didn't have a close relationship. She was close to her older sister, who had recently graduated from the University of Virginia and landed a job in environmental technology in West Virginia. She loved to visit her on her organic farm.

They got married the summer before he began law school. His parents wanted them to wait, but the two of them had their future all planned out. Julia started a nursing job and helped support them while he went for his law degree. Of course, he could have gotten financial help from his family, but they wanted to do it on their own. After all, his family was paying his law school tuition.

What had happened to that Julia of long ago? He wondered. They were so much in love.

Their life together progressed according to their plan. After he passed the bar, his father made sure he got a job with one of Cincinnati's most prestigious law firms and they moved into a beautiful house. Julia was more than happy to give up her career to help advance his. She desperately wanted a child, but she had a hard time getting pregnant. After years of trying and the best fertility doctor money could buy, they were finally blessed with their daughter Krista.

Julia was so happy then. She was a born mother. Her whole life centered around their daughter. Those were the good years. He became a full partner and quickly, with the right political backing, became a judge. They were on the A-list, leading a charmed life, when it all started to crumble.

When Krista left to attend the best finishing school for young women, his wife was completely lost. They argued about her going back to work, resuming her career in nursing. He had to put his foot down. He needed her to keep up with their social standing and nursing did not provide the picture he wanted to portray. He was hoping for a senate seat. How could they change their lifestyle when there was so much at stake? This is what they had planned. Their arguments became more and more heated. Kildeer recalled the night he came home to find her filling out an application to get recertified in nursing.

"I forbid it, I won't pay for this silly Florence Nightingale fantasy! You're the wife of a judge and hopefully a senator. I need you to do your part."

"You, you. It's always all about you! I need to have something of my own. Something fulfilling. I need something of my own."

He became enraged. He grabbed the form from her desk and tore it up. "Something of your own! What do you call this home, the very clothes you wear, the jewelry, the privileged lifestyle you enjoy?"

Julia was crying. "It's not enough. Don't you see? It's not enough. I'm nothing"

He was red with rage. "You are Judge David Paul Kildeer's wife and don't forget it, you spoiled, ungrateful bitch." He smacked her hard across the face. It wasn't the first time he'd struck her. Before, it came from his frustration—not a hard slap, just enough to show her who was boss—and was always followed by an apology. But this time it was an exercise of strength, a power he could use to control her. There would not be an apology.

She ran up to their bedroom and locked herself in. She didn't speak to him for weeks, just went through the motions of life like a robot, and he knew at once he had crossed a line. Things would never be the same again.

It was the night of the Cincinnati Symphony's big fundraiser; the press would surely be in attendance. She came down in a beautiful blue dress, her hair and makeup perfect—the bruise on her face well concealed.

"You look lovely," he commented. Julia walked over to the bar and poured herself a glass of scotch. No reply.

He noticed she was wearing the little gold heart necklace she had always worn in college.

"Why aren't you wearing your diamonds tonight?"

"I don't want to wear them." She took a couple of gulps of her drink.

"Put that drink down. You know you can't handle that so early in the evening. There will be plenty of drinks when we get there."

She placed the glass on the bar. She didn't look at him. "Whatever you say."

"And I say go up and put your diamonds on."

"And I say no!" she screamed.

He gave in, but he was seething all evening. Julia started downing drinks like the bar was going to close in ten minutes. She made a real spectacle of herself, slurring her words and laughing a bit too loudly. He grew more and more angry as the night wore on. But he held it in.

He went into their room as she was getting ready for bed. She didn't acknowledge that he was even in the room. He went wild. He ripped the heart necklace from her neck and threw it across the room. He started with one slap across the face. "Don't you ever embarrass me like that again!"

She put her hands across her throat. "Be careful, you might leave a bruise. Someone might notice what the wonderful Judge Kildeer is capable of. You might even end up in one of your own courtrooms." She turned her back on him, but he grabbed her and spun her around. He became a madman. He smacked her and then started punching her until she was in a ball in the corner whimpering. "Remember this, my darling Julia," he said before slamming the door. "You'll do as you're told. If you don't, I can have you destroyed."

And so, the vicious cycle began. She would pull herself together, go through the motions, then go on a drinking spree. He would erupt and smack her around. Their friends were beginning to notice that Julia had a drinking problem. That fit in with his narrative to friends that she fell down the steps, or had a car mishap. Eventually, when he felt he had enough sympathy from his friends, he would sadly divorce her. He needed to get their backing to keep custody of Krista.

He came home one night, not knowing what to expect. He called Julia's name, but no answer, which wasn't unusual. He went up to their bedroom to find her packing her clothes, all of them.

"What's this? Are you going on a trip?"

"I'm leaving, I can't live this way. I want a divorce." She didn't even look up, she just continued packing.

"Well, you're not getting one. Not until I'm ready. Not until I feel the time is right." He tried to keep his voice controlled even though he was boiling inside.

"Well, *I'm* ready. I can't take anymore. You're an animal who beats his wife and blames it on her drinking problem." She began to sob. "I just can't stand to live with you another minute. You disgust me!"

He saw the look of terror in her eyes as he pulled her away from the suitcase. "I disgust you?" he screamed. He dragged her over to the mirror. "Look at yourself! Tell me who is disgusting." He threw her across the room as she put her arms across her face and prepared for his blows. When he was done, she crawled into the corner and sobbed.

That was the end of it until her lawyer approached him at the club.

But he wouldn't let her get the best of him. No one got the best of Judge David Paul Kildeer!

"We'll be landing soon, sir. Please raise your drink tray."

The judge did as he was asked and handed the attendant his empty glass. He looked up and gazed into her face.

"Are you okay, sir?"

"Yes. You just remind me of someone I knew a long time ago."

* * * * *

The judge's flight arrived right on schedule, and after a short limo ride with an overly chatty driver he was seated at a quiet table in the back of the dining room, which was practically empty, just a few businessmen looking down at their cell phones while they ate. The judge recognized his old college roommate immediately and waved him over to the table. He stood up and embraced his old friend, noticing that he was solid muscle under his shirt. "You look great, Max. Fit as ever. I guess you have to stay in good shape in your line of work. Please, sit down. Let's get some drinks."

The first half hour they exchanged old fraternity stories. Through dinner they brought each other up to date on their careers.

"You've been leading quite an exciting life, my man," the judge stated as he took a bite of the chicken cordon bleu. "It makes mine seem very dull by comparison. I don't know if I could kill someone face to face. I don't know if I have what it takes."

"We all have it in us when we are in a kill-or-be-killed situation. I guess you get used to it eventually," Max stated flatly as he cut into his rare steak.

Don't press too hard, the judge thought to himself. "So, tell me, are you married, kids?"

"I was betrayed by two women in the same year. The 'company' sent a female to join me in the field. She didn't have the stomach for what we had to do to get information and she ratted me out to the chief. I was called in from the field. Not long after, my wife told me she wanted a divorce. She found someone else to share her lonely nights while I traveled. I guess I've had enough of women for a while."

The judge saw an entry but held back. "I know what you mean. My ex-wife got three million out of me when we divorced. I seriously thought about killing her for a while."

Max stared at him in amazement. "Three million! She robbed you blind. I can't say that I blame you for wanting to get revenge."

The judge changed the subject to UC football and the Cincinnati Bengals. Max still kept track of how the teams were doing, and asked questions about Cincinnati in general, remembering all of the bars they frequented in their college days. The judge filled him in on all of the renovations going on in the city. He described the Over-the-Rhine area and how popular that section of the city had become, especially the renovated park in front of Music Hall.

As the evening came to a close, the judge threw some bait. "So, I understand OCTOPUS has shut down for a while. Do you know how long until they reorganize?"

"I wish I knew. I can't stand sitting around much longer. I am used to a lot of action."

"Well, I may have something I can throw your way in a month or two if you're interested." He motioned to their waiter for the check.

"I may be. I'm afraid I am rusty on a lot of skills. Most of my job has been covert, a lot of killing." Max made the statement as if he were giving the time of day.

"Check back with me if things don't open up for you soon." The judge felt that when Max was desperate, he might agree to the task.

The judge thought about giving him his business card, but decided that would be too risky. There could be nothing on paper to connect the two old friends.

"This might be right up your alley."

21
A DRINK IN THE BAR

The ex-CIA agent decided to go to the bar for a nightcap after the judge left the restaurant; he dreaded going back to his empty apartment so early. He entered the dimly lit bar, which was a replica of an Irish pub. Dart boards graced the walls beside pictures of Irish poets.

He sat at the highly polished wood bar and ordered an Irish beer. "Looks like I'm your only customer tonight."

"Yeah, weeknights tend to be slow around here," the bartender said as he placed a beer in front of Max and walked to the end of the bar where a television was turned to a sports station.

David Kildeer hadn't changed a bit, Max realized. He was still the controlled, arrogant, entitled person he was back in college. It was no surprise he was now a judge, an expected outcome for someone with his pedigree.

Max had the distinct feeling that Kildeer had an underlying agenda. He made no mention of any "meeting with lawyers" he had mentioned in his phone call. Max's spy instincts told him there was more to the judge's visit than just wanting to catch up... much more. He sipped on his beer and re-ran their meeting through his mind. The judge had actually said he had thought about killing his wife after she took him for three million bucks. Max wondered what work Kildeer might offer him. He rubbed his forehead as if to clear his mind and took another sip from the green bottle. As he placed his beer down on the bar, he remembered his old friend's comment that he didn't think he could kill someone. The light went on. The agent's lips curled into a knowing smile. That could be it! He had a feeling that he knew what Kildeer was going to offer him. What did he say? "This may be right up your alley." Perhaps, the honorable judge wanted to hire him to eliminate his wife. This could be very lucrative, very lucrative. Time will tell. Time will tell. Patience, Max, patience....

The bartender walked by and glanced at the empty bottle. "I'll have another," Max nodded.

"Make that two." An attractive blonde sat down on the stool next to him. "Mind if I join you?" She wore a very seductive perfume. Just enough to tantalize her victim.

"Here you go, Gloria." The bartender smiled as he placed a beer in front of the blond.

Max turned and looked at her. "Not at all. I am all alone tonight." He had killing on his mind. He lifted his beer. "Cheers."

"Cheers," she replied in a throaty voice. "I'm Gloria. Who are you?"

"Otto," he lied as his eyes traveled down her neck, thinking how easy it would be to caress that milky-skinned throat, starting at her chin line, moving down slowly toward her soft shoulders and then gently squeezing it with his bare hands. He could feel the pleasure of squeezing harder and harder.

"That's a name you don't hear very often. What brings you to Little Rock? Business?"

She leaned on the bar in a way that made it easy to see down the V-neck pulled taut by her bulging breasts.

"I actually live here. I just met an old college friend while he was passing through on business. We hadn't seen each other in years." *Man, this chick is just asking for it.* He could rape and strangle her within the next two hours then get rid of her body and no one would be the wiser. She didn't know who she was messing with.

"Nothing like old friends." She ran her tongue over her lips after she took a sip of beer.

She seems to be known in this establishment. This must be her territory to pick up Johns. Stupid whore, you don't know who you're picking up. You're picking up Max the master. Max the torturer. Max the killer!

Her bright red fingernails tapped on the side of the glass. "What's your line of work?"

She's trying to find out what kind of money I have. They're all the same. He thought about all the women he picked up in sleezy bars when he was working out of the country. *They were all looking for a meal ticket or a one way ride out of their shithole countries.* "I'm a government contractor. I work overseas most of the time. I'm between projects right now. I get kind of restless when I'm not working. I'm used to more excitement." He winked as he emphasized the word excitement. "What do you do?"

"I'm an unemployed singer." Her full lower lip jutted out in a pout as she answered.

"Is that so? I guess it's hard to find steady work in that field." *I bet I could make you sing, sing for mercy, you money-grubbing bitch.*

Max felt her shoe move up and down against his leg as she expounded on the ups and downs of her music career and how she had to pick up extra work. *You stupid pig, I can make you regret coming on to me.*

"What kind of extra work?" Max asked as he ran his hand across her thigh, picturing what was beneath her clinging dress—obviously not underwear.

"I have an exciting treatment for loneliness and restlessness." A soft smile crossed her face. "And it's not very expensive." Her voice became softer and throatier. "One treatment usually does the trick, but some of my clients think they need more than one." She ran her finger across his lips. "I have an excellent cure record."

"I bet you do." His hand traveled further up her dress. "Where do you perform this miracle treatment? I don't have a room here." *There is no way I'm springing for a room for this bimbo.* "Can you administer your medicine in the car?" he asked in a low, sexy voice.

Gloria shrugged and rolled her heavily made-up eyes as she contemplated her options. "I guess so, but it will be more expensive without the luxury of an office. I have overhead, you know."

"What's the cost? I can probably cover it." *You won't get a dime from me, you pathetic bitch.*

"Six hundred. But I give a discount for follow-up treatments. I will make it worth your while."

Max hesitated a moment and then took the bait. "Let's go to my car. I'll pay for the drinks." He dropped some cash on the bar, not wanting to use a traceable credit card. As Gloria slithered off the barstool, Max's head filled with thoughts of all the delicious things he was going to do to her.

"I have to use the powder room. I'll meet you out front." She grabbed her purse and, propelled by her swaying hips, made her way to the restroom.

As he walked outside, the fresh air was like a slap to his face. He began to realize how risky this could be. The bartender could ID him. Max gave himself a lecture: No killing without a plan. That could ruin his prospects for the future. He was afraid he wouldn't be able to stop with just sex tonight. There would be a time for more kills but not now. He needed to be disciplined. It was all about patience; patience and control.

He climbed into his van and drove away just as Gloria came through the revolving door.

22
PHOTOGRAPHS

Gwen followed the black pick-up truck from a safe distance. They had been on I-75 north for two and a half hours. She talked with Zeke and Jack off and on as she traveled past the flat farmlands and small towns of central Ohio. When she spied the truck taking an exit that had no restaurant or motel signs she stayed as far behind as she could without losing them. They turned right off the main road. She slowed down and didn't turn right away, hoping she could catch up with them. There was a sign with "Hunter's Glen" printed in gold against a dark green background. Gwen crept along the road, hoping to spot them. Suddenly there was a dirt road marked with an arrow pointing left with "1 ½ miles to Zigler's Cabin" painted on it. She inched the car along for about a mile and spotted the black truck parked in front of a cabin. Slowly, she backed up and parked near the turn off. With heart pounding in her chest, she took a minute to collect her thoughts. She was terrified, but she had to figure out what connection Mark had to Charlie. Both were abusers and one was stalking his ex-wife. She had that same gut feeling she had about Julia's death.

She tried to draw on the courage she found when she confronted Brandon. She took several deep breaths and decided she would be very careful. It helped to realize Zeke was tracking her phone. She reached for her field glasses and placed the zoom lens on her camera.

Pulling the phone from the charger, Gwen took pictures of her surroundings and sent them to Zeke with a text. "It will be dark in about a half an hour. I am going to slip into the woods and then get closer for more pictures." After she turned the ringer off on the phone, she could feel it vibrating with Zeke's protest as she stuffed it into her pocket and slowly crept into the woods. She took more shots of the black truck and the four other vehicles parked outside the cabin, hoping to get a clear reading of the license plates. Gwen focused her field glasses at the main window of the cabin. Several men were walking around with drinks in their hands. Other than Mark and Charlie, she didn't recognize any of them.

The sun finally dropped below the tree line. Slowly she crept to the edge of the trees, every sound under her feet was amplified by fear. Gwen started making her way through a clearing to the side of the cabin but realized that was way too risky. She dashed back to the edge of the woods and hid behind some tall brush. She zoomed in with her camera and took a new picture every time someone was within the frame of the window. Finally, someone came right up to the window and looked out. She took a photo as quickly as she could. Then he lowered the shade.

The eerie night sounds of the forest were really freaking her out. With the aid of her phone flashlight, she groped her way through twigs and thorns until she reached her car. Gwen jumped in, started the engine and put it into gear. She glanced out her side window and gave a shriek. There was a man's face staring in at her.

Stay calm, think fast, she thought. She powered the window down halfway, keeping her other hand on the horn. "I am so sorry, you scared me half to death!"

"I was driving by and saw the light from your phone. Do you need some help? It's kind of late to be out here by yourself."

"Oh, no, I'm okay." She noticed the stranger looking at the camera in the passenger's seat. "I was out here earlier today taking pictures of birds. I'm a Photographer for *Wildlife Magazine*. The Scarlet Tanager is migrating through here right now. It's really quite beautiful, but of course you're not interested in that. Stupid me, I laid this expensive camera on the side of the woods while I was calling my boss to tell him I got a photo of one and drove off without it. As soon as I realized I left it I came back and used my cell phone flashlight to find it. I don't mind telling you it's a little creepy out here after dark."

She gave the stranger a smile and used her sweetest voice. "I so appreciate you stopping, but everything is okay." She made a mental note that he wore a green cap bearing the Hunter's Glen logo.

"Well, I'm sure glad about that. Do you know the way back out to the road?" He seemed to have swallowed her lies.

"I do. Thank you for stopping." She closed the window and locked her trembling hands on the steering wheel as she watched the stranger get back in his truck. Gwen gave him the sweetest smile she could muster with a little wave and drove out to the main road.

Once out of his sight she hit the accelerator until she reached the entrance ramp to I-75. At the next exit she stopped and filled up the gas tank and made an urgent trip to the restroom. She bought a soda and popped it open as she called Zeke.

"I'm on my way back to the office. I've got pictures."

"I'll meet you there," he yelled into his phone and abruptly disconnected.

"Well, he doesn't sound very happy," she said aloud as she turned on the radio to a light rock station and headed back to Cincinnati.

ANNETTE LACKNER

23
LIST

His handpicked jury had all arrived and were milling around the great room of the cabin. He threw another log on the fire as they helped themselves to the catered sandwiches the judge had picked up at his favorite up-scale deli on his way out of town. It took two years for him to put the plan together, including asking an associate for the use of his cabin once a month to go "hunting" with a group of his friends. His plan was unfolding like clockwork. The judge banged his gavel to let them know that their mock court was in session. The guests went to their assigned chairs. He passed out the "docket" and began to speak.

"Before we begin, we want to welcome Charlie. Charlie, I'm sure Mark has reiterated our rules to you. Go about your life as usual, keep your nose clean and above all absolutely no contact with your ex-wife or anyone who knows her. Got it?" The judge was a little wary of getting a new person involved, but when one of the original twelve dropped dead of a heart attack, he had to replace him. He had to have twelve, exactly twelve, including himself.

Charlie adjusted himself in his chair. "Sure, I got it, sir," he said, thinking, *What he doesn't know won't hurt him.*

"Okay, let us begin." Judge Kildeer passed out eleven sheets of paper. "Things are progressing quite well. We will now have a report from Max."

As the lumbering man stood up the judge recalled when Max finally took the bait. It was about three months after their original meeting when he got the call he had been waiting for. They met at the same hotel restaurant in Little Rock.

Max got right down to business. "So, what kind of opportunity do you have to offer? It doesn't look like OCTOPUS is going to regroup for quite a while."

The judge had sat back and sipped on his scotch. "First I need you to swear that all of this discussion is kept confidential whether or not you accept the job."

"You have my word." Max had been radiating a tingle of excitement. He had seemed to know he was about to be offered a position that was not run of the mill. Something clandestine, something "right up his alley."

The judge's tone had been matter of fact. "I told you I wanted to kill my wife. I'm prepared to pay you a handsome sum to do it for me."

Max had responded with silence. "Why me?" he finally asked.

The judge had appealed to Max's vanity. "Because you are the master. You would know how to accomplish it without getting caught. I have total trust in you to get the job done. Your reputation precedes you."

"Well, you're right about that," Max had replied, proudly. "I am a master. I could accomplish the deed without getting caught or implicating you."

The judge had filled Max in on the whole plan: twelve murders for $5 million.

As the judge expected, Max was unable to resist the kills, the excitement that was missing from his new life. He carefully gave Max the impression that as a judge, he had the money and power to fix any problems along the way.

And when he told Max he could plan and execute the mission in whatever manner he desired, he bit like the bloodhound he was, just as the judge expected.

Max said he would treat each woman as a separate mission, taking great pains to come up with the exact time, place and manner for each kill.

Yes, the plan is going forward just as I planned, the judge thought. He made sure his ex-wife was the first to go. Her elimination went without a hitch. He was upset with the local papers for printing her picture with the death notice—the less out there, the better. The good news was that all of Julia's estate went to Krista, which meant he hadn't expended the money at all. It was still in the Kildeer family. *The joke is on you, Julia,* the judge thought with a contented smile on his face.

His attention came back to the present as Max began to give his report.

"Well, as you know, Julia and Maura have been taken care of with no problems. You can now cross Gina off your lists."

The panel, obediently, did as they were instructed.

Max gave a quiet laugh, remembering how easy it was to take the jogger out. "Half of the women in Cincinnati are scared to death about the lurking strangler. There are no clues to be found. I decided on Meg next, because she is in Michigan and I thought the next murder shouldn't be local. I will use a completely different method, so no pattern can be detected."

Charlie was surprised since he was so late getting into the game. He wondered how in the hell this guy had already located Meg. He was reassured by the fact that this guy must be really good. Mark, on the other hand, was disappointed. His ex was on the bottom of the list. Once the plan had gotten underway, he began to crave the revenge he so desperately needed to be whole again.

The judge said, "Thanks, Max. Before we go any farther, I will ask as I always do, is everyone still in? No second thoughts of any kind?"

The eleven men exchanged solemn glances and nodded in assent.

The judge smiled a broad, fatherly smile. "Okay then, besides Meg we have eight other names. Will you supply Max with any information that he may need to execute our plan before we adjourn? And, as always, please destroy your notes before you leave in the morning."

The men looked down at their lists. They wanted to know who was left to condemn.

Meg
Jackie
Suzanne
Phyllis
Amy
Linda
Nancy
Patricia
Gwen

24

ZEKE'S PLAN

They were both standing behind Zeke's desk. Zeke and Jack. They didn't look welcoming.

"What the hell did you think you were doing?" Zeke yelled. "We were worried sick about you. Jack here was calling me every fifteen or twenty minutes to see what was happening. This was way too dangerous for you to take on alone." Zeke began circling his desk like an angry bull. "Don't you ever do this again! Someone should have been with you. What if they knew they were being tailed? It could have gotten rough!"

Jack stood up and opened his arms to her. "Not to mention a perfectly wonderful chicken marsala drying out on warm in my oven."

Gwen rushed to Jack and hugged him. "I'm so sorry I ruined dinner. I sort of got carried away in the moment." She tried to hide her irritation that these men didn't think she could take care of herself, but it did feel nice and safe to have Jack's arms around her.

Zeke, still fuming, continued. "I did some checking while you were up to your tricks. The cabin is owned by August Ziglar, the former congressman. The truck license is registered to your ex-husband, Mark, but we already knew that. I'll run a check on the other three cars. Let's see your other pictures."

Gwen got out her camera. "I don't know what we've got, I just kept clicking." She pulled the SD card from her camera, plugged it into her computer and downloaded the pictures.

The three huddled around the monitor. The pictures showed five men, two of whom were Charlie and Mark. The other three were a mystery. They kept looking and looking at the pictures for some other clues. "Who is that in the background?" asked Zeke, squinting his eyes. "Enlarge it a little more." Gwen and Jack looked at him as he studied the man. The suspect's face was mostly turned away from the camera, but Zeke continued to study it.

"Gwen, go get the envelope marked 'Meg Watkins' that's laying on my desk, please."

Gwen rooted through the files spread out on Zeke's desk and handed the envelop to him. Her boss pulled out pictures from the folder and shuffled through them. Finally, he picked one out from the rest and stared at it. "I can't be sure, but there is a resemblance." He held the picture up to Jack and Gwen. "Can you see it?"

Gwen studied the photo. "Oh my God, yes," she whispered. She tried to ignore the shiver traveling up her spine.

"Who is it?" Jack couldn't tell anything.

Gwen looked at Jack, her eyes wide in disbelief. "It's a man who was hanging out around the missing girl Meg's house in Michigan."

Zeke began to pace around the office, his hand rubbing his chin. "Okay, I have to organize my thoughts and check out the other cars. We also need to check out that cabin. Let's all go home and meet back here at ten tomorrow morning. We'll be able to think much clearer after a little rest." He looked at the two of them. "That's not too early is it? I almost forgot that there is love in bloom here."

Gwen gave him a sarcastic look. "We'll be here at 10."

· · · · ·

Jack and Gwen stopped by Gwen's place and fed a cantankerous Ethel, then went to Jack's place for a very late-night dinner.

"I'm starving," Gwen said. "All that excitement gave me a ravenous appetite." She was setting the table while Jack took the chicken out of the microwave and grabbed a beautiful salad out of the fridge. He placed the food on the table and took her in his arms. "And all of that worrying gave me an appetite too, but not for food." He kissed her behind her ear.

Gwen sat down at the table and pointed to his chair. "First things first." She started serving their salads. Even though it was a bit dry they gorged themselves on the chicken.

"Gwen, please don't take chances. Listen to Zeke. Now that I've found you, I don't want to lose you."

Gwen dug her fork into the last piece of chicken on her plate. "I am sorry I worried you, Jack. I just got carried away in the moment." She pushed her plate away. "Let's go to bed and I'll make it up to you."

They left the dishes in the sink and went to his bedroom and the comfort of each other's arms.

* * * * *

At 10:00 sharp, Gwen and Jack entered the office carrying a bag of donuts and three coffees. Zeke looked up. "Thanks for picking up breakfast. I came in a couple of hours ago." He grabbed the coffee, took a sip, and plunged his hand into the bag of donuts. "I did a tracer on the other three cars and guess what? Two of them were registered to spouse abusers, the third was a rental from Bargain Auto. I can't get any information from them because of privacy laws, but I have a feeling it was probably rented by our mystery man. I also found out something very interesting. One of the cars is registered to Ralph DeAngelo, the ex-husband of the woman who was killed in Chicago. The problem is he has an air-tight alibi for the night of the murder."

Gwen took in a deep breath. "So, we have four known abusers and a man we believe is stalking an ex-wife. I just know Judge Kildeer has something to do with this. He was an abuser. Julia died in a car accident and her sister thinks he is involved somehow. But he doesn't show up in my pictures."

Zeke scratched his balding head. "That doesn't mean he wasn't there. We just don't have any evidence that he was."

Jack stood up and started pacing. "I can go on the court website and try to find out if these men had any link to Kildeer. I still have my attorney's license, so I should be able to access some of the court files."

Zeke walked over to the window and looked outside. "I have another idea if you two are game. The cabin is listed on VRBO. Zigler rents it out through an agency. If we can get access to the cabin, maybe we can find some clue as to what was going on there the other night. But we need to get in as soon as possible. Hopefully, the dumpster is still full so we can go through the garbage. Jack, can you go on the website and rent it as soon as possible? I don't want to use my credit card or anything that could trace back to me."

Jack sat down at Gwen's computer, then had a change of heart. "Let me drive home and do it from my personal computer. I'll see what I can find out in the court records while I'm at it. I don't want anything traced back to you or Gwen."

"Great, let me know what you set up, I'll be ready at the drop of a dime. Let's call it a day, kids."

Zeke walked to the door with them and locked up the office.

25
JACK

The house felt like a tomb without Gwen there. It was the same way he felt when Kay died. He would come home to an empty house still expecting to see her there, sitting at the dining room table surrounded by legal documents, her auburn hair hiding her face as she bent over the computer. She was so brilliant. She shared her love of the law with him. That was why he finally gave up their practice. It was never the same without Kay, his beautiful Kay.

He fondly remembered when he met her. They were both in law school and shared classes. They kept running into each other everywhere. Soon they fell in love and moved in together. They were poor as church mice, but as happy as they ever were. When Kay became pregnant with Joe, she took it right in stride, continuing with her studies. They both landed jobs with firms in Cincinnati and after years of hard work they had enough saved to go into practice on their own. The couple loved the Queen City. It had a small town feeling but offered the same perks of a big city. It provided a first-class symphony, a ballet company and a variety of museums. They took advantage of the fabulous county park system and spent many hours hiking and boating when Joe was small. Their life, although demanding, was almost perfect until her fatal diagnosis.

When hospice came to take care of his failing wife, he walked around the house like a ghost. He was helpless and found the only thing he could do was put up a strong front for Joe and sit at her side holding her hand.

"I know you don't want to hear it," he could hear her whispering, "but I want you to get married again someday. I want you to know you have my blessing. You're too young to be alone."

He recalled telling her with tears trickling down his face, "I'll never find anyone like you."

Jack realized that he hadn't found anyone like Kay. He also now understood how someone could fall so completely in love again. Gwen wasn't Kay. She was quirky and refreshing. She didn't see the strength in herself that Jack could recognize. She was a woman who had reached deep down inside and found the courage to survive.

He smiled as he cleaned up the dishes they had left from last night and this morning, when lovemaking was much more important than a few dishes in the sink. "God, I hate this empty house," he said to himself.

Jack sat down on the sofa with his laptop, logged on to VRBO and put in a request for the area they wanted. There it was. It looked like a very nice retreat. He went through the options to see the next available date, which was tomorrow night. Jack signed for everything and got instructions on how to get to the agency office for the keys.

A few glasses of wine later, he was still searching through the court records of each of the abusers identified by Gwen's photos. Yes, they were all abusers sued by their ex-wives. They all had served some time, and after being paroled, had to attend anger management classes. He looked at the dates of the court filings. They were over a period of 13 years. The oldest file belonged to Mark. His anger rose as he read about what Mark had done to Gwen. "What kind of animal could beat up a pregnant woman?" he asked himself. He studied and studied the documents, and just as he was about to shut down the computer and turn on the 11:00 o'clock news, it jumped out at him. He found the connection, the link that tied these men together.

He sent off a text to Zeke and Gwen and told them they would go to the lodge tomorrow night. He had posed as a husband whose father-in-law from Indiana wanted to visit, so he and his wife were going to meet him halfway, so "dad" didn't have to drive too far. Jack rented it for two nights.

Then he shared the really big news. The presiding judge on all of these cases was none other than

Judge David Paul Kildeer.

ANNETTE LACKNER

26
A VISIT WITH DAD

The rental office was in a small cottage next to a playground and swimming pool for use by summer guests. Gwen panicked when she realized that the man at the desk was the same person who stopped to help her outside of the cabin. She immediately ducked behind a rack of postcards, pretending to be interested in the local sites. When the middle-aged, balding man looked up, Jack took the lead and began to fill out the paperwork.

"Oh, Dad, can you check the license plate numbers from your rental car?" he asked. Zeke had rented a car just across the state line in Indiana to keep up the ruse that he came from Indiana. He peeked out the door and recited the numbers. Just as the clerk gave Jack the keys he glanced over to Gwen. "Hey, aren't you the one who was out in the dark retrieving a camera the other night?"

Gwen's heart jumped into her throat as she emerged from behind the rack of cards. "Yes, I am." She looked at her partners. "This gentleman was kind enough to pull over and make sure I was alright." She tried to signal them through her tone of voice. "In fact, that's when I thought that this would be the ideal location to meet Dad. Jack went on VRBO and here we are. It worked out perfectly." She flashed a big toothy smile at the clerk.

Zeke picked up the signal. "Yeah, it is perfect. I can't drive as long as I used to. It gets to my back."

"Housekeeping was in today, so you have plenty of fresh towels and starter items in the kitchen. If you need anything else just give us a call. Someone will be here until 6:30.

Will you be photographing birds for your magazine again?"

Gwen smiled her sweetest smile. "No, I'm on vacation with my dad. But if I see an opportunity for a fabulous shot, I might change my mind."

"Well, enjoy your visit. It's one of our nicest cabins. Nothing but the best for Mr. Zigler. He's a retired congressman, you know. Most of our owners are top-notch people."

Zeke bristled. "Well, that's good to know. We wouldn't want any riffraff around. Let's go get settled in, kids."

Jack started the car and Zeke gave Gwen a severe look. "What the heck was that all about? You didn't say anything about someone seeing you the other night."

Gwen explained what happened, trying to play down the whole episode.

Zeke gave her a stern fatherly look. "I don't like him being able to connect you with the group who was here the other night. That could prove to be dangerous."

They unlocked the door and checked out the cabin, then brought in their bags and food supplies. "He wasn't kidding when he said it's nice," Jack commented as they looked around. "What a great fireplace. The whole place looks like a top decorator designed it. And what a kitchen! We'll cook up some magic tonight."

Jack started to pile some wood into the fireplace. "Wait, wait." Zeke went over and pulled the wood out. "Let's check out the grate for any remnants that might hold a clue."

He grabbed the poker and pushed around the ashes, but found nothing. "Okay, go for it."

Within an hour the three of them were sitting around a blazing fire with glasses of wine.

"So, what's our agenda, Zeke?" Gwen sat in an overstuffed chair with her feet curled up under her.

"First, let's go over what we think we are looking at here. We have a group of men supposedly on a hunting weekend. We know that there were four known abusers present and perhaps the man who is stalking Meg in Michigan. Jack has linked them all to Judge Kildeer, but we don't know if the judge was here or not. We do know that his wife was killed in a suspicious accident, and we also know that the ex-husband of the woman killed in Chicago, Maura Di Angelo, was here. The problem is he has an alibi. We don't know for sure that Julia Kildeer was murdered, and we are not sure of the stranger in the photo. So, for the next hour or so, let's go through this place with a fine-toothed comb. Just the tiniest thing might be important. Tomorrow morning I'll see if there is anything in the dumpster." The detective arose from his chair and clapped his hands together. "Let's get to work, team."

They searched everywhere, under the beds, in the drawers, the bathroom cabinets, behind furniture. Nothing. The housekeeper had done a good job... too good. Zeke went up to the well-stocked bar and picked the lock. He took out the three bottles in the front and dusted them for fingerprints then lifted them off onto a piece of tape. "It probably won't turn up anything, but you never know."

Disappointed that they hadn't found anything yet, they decided to have dinner and get back to work after their stomachs were filled. Jack grilled steaks on the front porch while Gwen put potatoes in the oven and prepared a salad.

After dinner, Zeke turned on his laptop and downloaded Gwen's pictures. He stood by the picture window to get the camera's perspective. "It looks like someone was leading a discussion. You can see how everyone in these photos was looking toward the fireplace, perhaps at the chair you have been sitting in, Gwen."

She felt a tingle of fear travel from her head right down to her toes, knowing that a killer may have sat in the same chair. "Do you think it was some kind of a meeting?"

"I think so. We have to find out if Kildeer was here. He seems like the logical one to lead a meeting."

They spent the remainder of the evening sitting by the fire and talking. Zeke stood up. "Well, old 'Dad' here is going to turn in. The two of you sleep tight tonight." He made his way upstairs to his room and closed the door, wanting to give his companions some privacy.

Jack and Gwen curled up in each other's arms. "I can't wait," said Jack as he kissed the top of Gwen's head and placed his hand inside her sweatshirt.

"Wait for what?" She pressed her body against him.

"I was going to say I can't wait until we are married and living under the same roof. But the way I'm feeling now, I can't wait to get you to the bedroom."

Gwen stood up and pulled him by the hand. "You don't have to wait. It's right down the hall." He followed her to the main bedroom and pulled down the shades. By the time he turned around Gwen was in bed naked waiting for him. She patted the bed. "What's taking you so long?" With that he was in bed, pulling her next to him. "I love you," he whispered.

. . . . .

Gwen heard Jack get up and throw on his jeans and sweatshirt. The lovely smell of fresh brewed coffee filled the air. She rolled over and stretched out her arms. "I'm so warm and cozy, I don't want to get up."

"I'll get you some coffee." Jack bent down and kissed her.

She smiled up at him. "You know you're spoiling me. I'm going to expect this every morning."

He kissed her again and went out to the kitchen.

Zeke was nowhere to be found, so Jack pulled on his jacket and went out on the porch, where he found the detective having a smoke.

"Good morning, Jack. I found a dumpster on the side of the cabin. I was just about to see if there is anything in it. If there is, I'll bring the bags into the cabin so we can go through them."

"Have at it. I'm going to grab a cup of coffee for the two of us. We'll help you go through it."

Gwen was already up and dressed when he went into the kitchen. "I thought you wanted coffee in bed?" Gwen looked like a teenager in her jeans and UC sweatshirt. Her skin was shiny and fresh without makeup.

"I was afraid coffee in bed might lead to something else in bed." She pushed her finger into his chest. "We've got work to do today, pal."

They sat down at the rugged pine table and sipped their coffee in the sunlight that streamed through the window. They almost forgot for the moment the reason they were in the cabin.

"Well, well sleeping beauty is finally up," commented Zeke as he pushed his way through the door, carrying three bulging trash bags. Jack jumped up to help him bring them into the kitchen area. Zeke grabbed a couple of fresh trash bags from under the sink and spread them out on the table. "Okay, let's see what we've got here." He poured the contents out onto the table.

Little by little they combed through the trash: lots of food wrappers, empty cigarette packs, paper plates and plastic cups. They scoured through all three of them. Nothing.

"Well at least we gave it the old college try." Jack started putting the contents back into the bags.

"Someone forgot to recycle this," Jack said, holding up a beer can. "Is there a recycling bin anywhere?"

"There's probably one on the back porch. I'll put these back and check it out," Zeke said.

Jack opened the door for him and went back to Gwen, who was pouring a second cup of coffee. "Zeke makes a mean cup of coffee." She placed the warm cup between her palms and took a sip.

A few minutes later their companion returned from the backdoor. "It was in the back. You want to help me go through it? You never

ANNETTE LACKNER

know." He handed them each a pair of plastic gloves. They sat on the back deck in the chilly air, going through the contents.

"The Bud drinker has a habit of crushing the center of his can before he pitches it."

Jack held a bent aluminum beer can out for the others to see.

"Habits are good, they usually lead to clues. Let's try to dust a few of the cans for fingerprints. In fact, let's take some with us in case we can get some DNA from them."

Gwen pulled out eight or ten Bud cans out of the pile. "Do you just want any of them, or certain ones?"

"Why don't we take all of them so I can go through them at home." Zeke went into the kitchen and got a trash bag to transport the cans home in his car.

They spent the rest of the day just relaxing. Jack and Gwen took a long hike in the woods, while Zeke had a few "brewskies" in front of the TV, watching whatever sports he could find.

After eating hot dogs and hamburgers cooked on the grill, they pulled a Scrabble box off the game shelf. After two games, the trio settled in to watch a film on the old movie channel, sipping beer and wine and munching on popcorn.

"I'm going to get an early start tomorrow," Zeke said as he took his dirty dishes into the kitchen and rinsed them out. "I want to see if I can get something off those beer cans, and I have an idea on how to find out if Judge Kildeer was here."

"How are you going to do that?" Gwen followed him with the rest of the dishes.

Zeke reached into his pocket and pulled out a pocketknife. "This little baby right here."

"It looks like a really nice one." Jack took it from his hand and examined the carved ivory handle. "This must have set you back a pretty penny."

"Actually, it was a gift from a friend."

Gwen was puzzling. "How does that fit in?"

"I'm going to stop in the resort office and tell them I found it. The previous renter must have left it. Maybe they will give me the address and I can mail it to him."

"Great idea." Gwen began to realize how good Zeke was at his job as she rinsed off the remaining dishes.

"We'll see what happens. Anyway, I'm leaving early, so no need for you two to get up. I'll put on the coffee. If I find out anything, I'll text you on the way out."

* * * * *

The office was just opening when Zeke pulled up.

The clerk looked up from a crossword puzzle book. "Well, how was your stay?"

"Just great, the cabin was top-of-the-line. I'm heading home, but my daughter and son-in-law will be there until 1:30. That's check-out time, right?"

"Yep. 1:30. Gives housekeeping a chance to get in there and give it a thorough cleaning." He took a sip from his thermal coffee mug.

"I think the previous renter must have left this behind." Zeke pulled the knife out of his pocket. "It's really an expensive one. If you have an address, I can see that it gets to him."

"Man, that's a nice pocketknife!" Chuck turned it over and over in his hands, examining the fine details carved into the ivory handle. "Thanks for being so honest and not taking it. No need for you to go to any trouble, he's here with some friends once a month. I'll see that he gets it." He placed the pocketknife in a basket on his desk marked "Lost and Found."

Zeke said good-bye and headed for the door, disappointed that his scheme had failed. "Well, thanks again for a nice weekend, I'd love to come back sometime."

"Our pleasure. And thanks for being honest. I'm sure the judge will appreciate it."

. . . . .

Gwen woke up early. Zeke had made the coffee, as promised. She poured a cup and looked out the window to a winter wonderland. There was a thin layer of snow on the ground—a beautiful wet snow that clung to the trees. The whole world looked new and untouched. She sipped her coffee and told herself, *that is how Jack makes me feel: new and untouched.* Something she never thought would be possible.

"A penny for your thoughts." Jack hugged her from behind.

"They're worth much more than that. I was just thinking how much I love you."

She turned and put her arms around him.

He went over to the counter and poured himself a cup of coffee and warmed hers. "How about we go back to bed." He poked his finger into her chest. "We *don't* have work to do today, pal."

They made love and cuddled under the down comforter, then fell back asleep. Gwen woke to the sound of her phone chirping to announce that she had a text. She looked at the time. 11:30 a.m. She sat up and shook Jack. "Wake up, we need to clean up and pack."

Jack stretched and put his hand on her leg. "I was hoping it was a blizzard and we were shut in for two or three days."

Gwen sat up on the edge of the bed. "Oh my God, I just got a text from Zeke. All that it says is,

'JUDGE WAS HERE!'"

27
ZEKE

"What on earth are you doing?" Margie stood there with her hands on her hips looking at the array of empty beer cans strewn across her kitchen table. Zeke was dusting them off with a dark powder and then placing a piece of clear packaging tape over each print he could see. Then he carefully lifted the tape and placed it on a vinyl square, cutting away the excess tape from the vinyl.

"Just doing my job. Sorry." He began examining the beer cans one by one. "I have to get these over to Mike at the department to check out the prints for a match."

As he looked them over, he noticed a cigarette stuffed in one or two of them. That could be a habit. He started looking down the open hole of each one. "Well, well, well, what have we got here?" A piece of yellow paper was folded up and stuffed inside one of the cans. "Margie, would you get me something I can poke in here to try to get this out?"

Margie rattled through her junk drawer and handed him a bamboo spear she used to make kebabs. "The things I do for love. Will this work?"

"Perfect. You're a doll, Margie." He slowly coaxed the paper through the hole and tugged it out, then unfolded it and laid it flat on the table. "It's a list of names." He continued to look through the blurred printing and stopped dead in his tracks. His heart jumped into his throat when he saw the printed names on the yellow paper. He read it over and over trying to convince himself this was real. The first on the list was "MEG," but most of the others were too smeared to read. Then the last one jumped out at him. Zeke gasped as he allowed himself to contemplate its implications. The letters spelled out very clearly: "GWEN."

28
PLAY IT SMART

"Morning, boss." Gwen pulled her chair up to Zeke's desk. "Okay, I can't wait. Tell me about what the clerk said when you checked out. Your text has me intrigued."

"Well, I don't know for sure that it is Kildeer, but it's the logical assumption. The clerk said he would give the knife to the previous renter, then called out to me as I was leaving the office, 'I'm sure the judge will appreciate it.' I'm almost sure it is our judge." Zeke looked worried. "Where's Jack? I need to talk to the two of you together."

Gwen noticed the grave sound of her boss' voice and wondered what caused his tone. "He'll be along, he had to clear some things up at his office. Do you have some ideas as to what we do next?"

"Let's wait for Jack," Zeke said.

A moment later Jack strolled through the door.

"Sit down, I need to talk to the two of you." Zeke motioned to the chairs beside his desk.

The couple sat down as told. They could tell something was wrong.

"I did lift a few fingerprints off the beer cans. I dropped them off to my pal at police headquarters, along with a mixture of beer cans. It's not likely, but maybe he can pick up some DNA. He's going to run the fingerprints through the database. But there's more. I found a paper inside one of them that had a list on it. There were nine names on it. The first one was Meg. We know three women are dead: Julia, Maura and Gina, but their names are not on the list. We have linked all of their husbands to Judge Kildeer and we also know Meg is being stalked, and I think I know why."

"Murder." Gwen said it in a hushed voice. She grabbed Jack's hand. "It's a list of women to murder."

"And if Meg's name is at the top of the list, that could mean she's next," Jack said. He put his hand on Gwen's shoulder.

The detective nodded his head. "Exactly. That's why I am going to Michigan to keep an eye on her house. If she's next, maybe I can stop it. I think our stranger may be a hired killer."

Gwen interrupted, "That's too dangerous! Can't you get help from the police?" She had visions of Julia burning up in her car, of Maura being strangled in her apartment and the jogger. Were they up against a brutal killer? She began to be very frightened for Zeke as her theories suddenly took the shape of cold-blooded facts.

"I don't have enough evidence to get their help. And I hope I am wrong, but I don't think I have any time to waste."

"Let me go with you, I can clear things up at work. I don't like the idea of you going alone." Jack began to pace.

"No, I need you to stay here and watch out for Gwen."

"I'm fine," Gwen snapped back in reply.

"No, you are not fine." Zeke paused. He hated to scare her, but knew he had to tell her. "Your name is at the bottom of the list."

Jack froze in place. "And that animal Mark was at the cabin. I'll kill him!"

Zeke held out his hands as if to calm Jack down. "None of that! We have to play this very smart. Getting upset won't help. You have to protect Gwen while I'm away."

Jack pulled back and composed himself. "Of course. I'll stay at her place until all of this is settled."

"Just go about your normal routine until I get back. But don't, under any circumstances, leave her out of your sight. I could be gone for several days. I'll keep you posted day by day. Be extremely vigilant. I think we're dealing with pure evil here."

29
RETURN TO MICHIGAN

It was the third day and still no sign of the stranger. Zeke was going through the various angles in his mind and felt pretty sure they were on to some kind of plot. He tried to put himself into the mindset of the known men who were involved, including the judge.

His cell phone rang displaying "GWEN."

"Hi, what's up, Gwen."

"Zeke, I think I've got it!" Her voice was breathless and excited.

"Yeah, go on."

"Well, last night I was reading through all of my 'abuse' manuals and it just hit me. The traits of abusers have been going over and over in my mind: excessive jealously, controlling, isolating, forcing sex, and rigid gender roles. The number-one reason women don't leave is because, in their minds, it is too dangerous."

"I know. Statistics show that abused women are more likely to be murdered in the first few weeks after they leave." Zeke said.

"Don't you see? The three dead women *did* leave. They had the guts to go to the police and then to court!"

"Hold on." Zeke glanced up through his windshield after hearing a sound—just a mailman on his route. Then he watched a figure down at the end of the street. It was a young mom walking her toddler. He returned to Gwen on the phone. "Go ahead."

"Zeke, these women left. They were strong women."

Zeke lit a cigarette and inhaled, lowering his window to allow the smoke to escape the car while Gwen continued in an excited voice.

"*That's it! They* dared to be strong, reversing the perceived gender roles. It would infuriate their spouses. I figure the judge was too smart to have anything done to Julia during the first year or so. He would be patient enough to wait for a little time to go by. If Julia settled out of court and agreed to keep it private, she probably got a large settlement. That would infuriate him, too."

Zeke smiled. "I think you are on to something. All of this leads to another question. What's in it for the others?"

"You're the detective. Figure it out."

"I plan to do just that. I've got to go now. Good work, Gwen. You're turning into a real detective."

He glanced up again. And there was the stranger strolling down the street, hands tucked into his pockets. His hair was no longer blond. It was almost black, the cut entirely different. It could even be a wig. Zeke put his newspaper in front of his face as the stranger strolled by. He stayed and sat there for hours, but the stranger didn't return. He watched the sun set behind the houses that were becoming very familiar to him. *That's okay,* he thought, *I'm a very patient man. As patient as a judge.*

30
WARNING

He sat in his chamber reviewing the day's docket. His eyes caught sight of a few file folders placed on the side table. He would have to remind his secretary again to be sure to put them in the wooden box in the corner. Why was it so difficult to get people to obey his directives? His cell rang and he was surprised to see it was the office clerk from the cabin.

"Hi, Chuck. Everything okay?" The judge glanced at the large round clock on the wall, always conscious of how much time he had to stay on his tight schedule.

The rental clerk leaned back in his chair and examined the item in his lost and found basket. "Just wondering if you left an ivory-handled pocketknife at the cabin. The last renters dropped it off when they left. Said they found it there."

The judge stiffened. "No… did they rent right after my friends and I were there?"

"Yeah, two days later. It was a couple and their father."

"Had they ever rented before?"

The clerk scratched his chin. "No, but the woman was here taking pictures of birds in the woods. I think it was the same day you came in last week."

Kildeer's interior alarm bell rang. Someone was around the cabin taking pictures when they had their meeting. "Chuck, you don't have any surveillance cameras around your rental office, do you? I've been getting some threats lately. Probably from someone who received a stiff sentence from me."

"What we have is one of those devices that signal your phone when there is someone at the door. I get a video on my cell. We had some vandalism here last summer. Just kids on a tear, nothing serious. I can see if someone approaches the building at night and get right over here. Let me check it out and try to text it to you. Will that work?"

Chuck felt a new sense of importance. After all, the judge was one of their most prestigious clients. If he was getting threats Chuck might be saving his life.

"That would be great. Text whatever you have to me. You'll find my gratitude in an envelope in your mailbox. Thanks again. Bye-bye," he said as he brushed a piece of lint off of his desk.

The judge sat back in his chair waiting for the familiar tone on his phone while he considered what his next move should be. He picked up the signaling phone and opened the text. There were three people outside the door; a man in his 60's, a very attractive blond who appeared to be in her 30's and a man who looked a few years older. It looked just like what Chuck described: a young couple and their dad. He enlarged it and studied it. The younger man looked slightly familiar. He would have to jog his memory and check him out, but right now he was due back in the courtroom to dispense justice.

31
DELIVERY TRUCK

He parked farther down the street today—day five—and so far, no sign of the stranger. After about an hour he decided to take a walk. The detective got out of the car and stretched, reached into the backseat and retrieved a parka and sock hat. The temperature had taken a real dive last night.

He strolled along a street adorned with all manner of Christmas decorations. The boughs of greens, the red bows, the toy soldiers, the Nativity Scenes all spoke of warmth and joy; everything he wasn't feeling right now. The decorations reminded him that he needed to get Margie a nice Christmas gift, perhaps one of those all-inclusive trips to an island in the sun. Zeke was sure Jack would help him plan something and possibly give him a good deal. He hoped this thing between Gwen and Jack worked out to be something lasting, for both of their sakes.

While Zeke was ambling down the street, Meg was in the kitchen making chili for dinner. It was her go-to comfort food. Whenever she was feeling homesick, she would make one of her mother's favorites. She went on-line and found a recipe close to what Clare would make and had been peeling onions and peppers and mincing garlic ever since. A tin of corn muffins was in the warmer. It would be a nourishing, tasty dinner for a cold day. Carly and Eli were due home in about 45 minutes. She turned the pot on low and started to set the table. They planned on watching *Rudolph the Red-Nosed Reindeer* and *Frosty The Snowman* on TV tonight while they strung popcorn for their tree.

Max drove the delivery van slowly down the street. He had been watching and knew Meg was working in the kitchen. The explosive device was activated for five minutes after he left the scene. Then he would place a call to Meg from All About Town Delivery Service that a Christmas Package had been left at the door. It would detonate as soon as the sensor recognized motion within four feet.

Thoughts flooded his memory of the 21 civilians in Afghanistan, the blood, the body parts scattered throughout the decimated building, the sheer carnage. *Of course, there is always a chance of collateral damage,* he thought. He decided this was the best method of removal for Meg. He moved her up on his list because she was living in Michigan. His kills, so far, were in different states; there were no connections. What could be more appropriate this time of year than a nice holiday package all tied up in ribbons, placed on the front porch?

Zeke stopped to text Gwen and Jack to make sure they were okay. As he looked up, he saw a white delivery van in Meg's driveway. The driver had set a beautifully wrapped package by the front door, a festive splash of silver and gold. As he got back into the van, he looked directly at Zeke and sped away. My God, it was the stranger! Zeke sprinted as fast as his 64 years would allow. His only thought was to get Meg out of the house. He ran to the backdoor and banged his fist on the door as hard as he could.

Meg heard the banging. She slowly made her way down the back hall to the door. She was afraid to answer. She could see an older man. He rammed his fist through the glass pane. She started to back away.

"I am a private detective hired by your mother," the intruder was yelling. "You've got to get out right now. There's a bomb on your front porch. GET OUT NOW!"

She paused not sure what she should do. Should she believe him?

Zeke could picture the timer counting down. Ten, nine, eight. "NOW"!

She followed her instincts and unlocked the door. He grabbed her by the arm, pulling her through the side yard toward the street. Her telephone was ringing in the background. "JUST RUN!" he shouted.

Just as they reached the curb, a car pulled in the driveway.

"Oh God, it's Carly and Eli," Meg wailed.

The little boy got out and started running toward the package on the front porch.

"NOOOOO, STOP!" Meg screamed as loud as she could.

Zeke flew across the yard and in one motion scooped Eli into his arms and ran. Then, a loud explosion before everything went black.

He came to, flat on his back. There was a horrible ringing in his ears.

"Are you all right?" Meg was bending over him. Her voice sounded far away. Carly was standing next to her holding Eli in her arms, crying. Zeke sat up, shaking his head. "I think so." Slowly he pulled himself up to a standing position. His arm hurt like the devil. He looked at it and realized some debris must have hit him. It didn't appear to be anything major.

"You saved our lives," Carly sobbed clinging to her wailing son. "If you hadn't thrown Eli, he could have been killed." He noticed blood coming from a cut above her eye.

He gave a quick assessment of the house. The whole porch was obliterated, and the front door was completely blown in. He turned around to see the street full of neighbors.

"The police and an ambulance are on their way," someone shouted.

"I think we're all okay," Zeke shouted back "Thanks. You can all go inside now. We'll keep you posted."

He led the three in through the back door. "I suggest we find a motel to stay in for tonight. I'll need to go back to Cincinnati tomorrow. Meg, your mother hired me to find you. I've been watching the house to make sure you were here and safe. Then I noticed this guy hanging around. He's the one who put the bomb on the front porch.

And I discovered your name was on a list at some kind of meeting your ex has been attending. I have a feeling it was a hit list."

Meg began to cry as she related the story of Charlie threatening her in the supermarket.

"He won't hurt my parents, will he?" A look of sheer terror was on her face.

Zeke tried to reassure her. "No, no. Don't you worry. I think the stranger will lay low now. Especially from your family. I need to clear a few things up on this case, so I'm going to ask you to wait until you get the okay from me before you call them. Can you do that?"

They heard the sirens and went to the gaping hole in the front door to greet them.

Not only were police and ambulance trucks arriving, but there were several local news station vans outside getting hooked up for an evening news report. The neighbors were back outside taking in the excitement.

The officers began placing yellow tape around the front of the residence, while the paramedics examined Eli and Carly. Meg told the police her story and Zeke gave updates on what he had been pursuing. He also told them he could ID the stranger and could fax them a picture. He told the officers he would drive to headquarters and talk to the person in charge of the case, but they insisted they all go to the hospital to get checked out first. While the police were investigating the scene, Zeke spotted Eli looking very frightened. *Poor kid. He's probably scared to death*, he thought. He took Eli by the hand. "It's okay, kid, it's okay." He walked him back into the kitchen and spotted the pot of chili on the stove and turned off the burner. "Hey, let's not let this go to waste. I'm starving." He picked up two chairs that had been blown over by the blast, put Eli on one of them and sat down on the other.

Meg joined them, drying her tears before she took the muffins out of the warmer. She began to ladle the chili into the bowls and broke down into uncontrollable sobs. Zeke ran over and put his arms around her. "There, there now, it's okay. Just let it all out. I promise we are going to get the son of a bitch who did this. And if Charlie had anything to do with it, we'll get him too."

Meg invited the paramedics to have some food while she and Carly packed up a few clothes. Zeke had a neighbor help him board up the front of the house, asking Eli to help them just to keep the bewildered tyke busy.

The impatient paramedics finally got them into the ambulance. Zeke threw a towel over his head to fake an injury, but in truth he didn't want his picture on any newscast. He had too much work ahead of him to be recognized by the wrong people.

Their minor injuries were treated, just a few stitches, but the doctors decided to keep them overnight for observation. When given the okay the police interviewed them again, each one separately.

Zeke was just about to call Margie when there was a soft knock on his half-opened door.

Eli ran to the detective, who was sitting on the edge of his bed, and gave him a hug around his legs. "You were a real super-hero today. Thank you for saving me."

"Nothing to it, Buddy." He ruffled the little boy's hair. "Now your job is to be a good boy and take good care of your Mom, okay?" Zeke looked at Carly and Meg standing in the doorway. They both mouthed the words "thank you."

When they went back to their rooms and Zeke was finally alone, he called Margie and filled her in on the events of the day.

"Oh my God, Zeke are you sure you're alright? You're not a young rookie anymore."

"Don't I know it, Margie. Not to worry, everything checked out okay. I'm just tired.

I think I'm getting too old for this shit. Right now, I just need a good night's sleep." He nodded off before he could even put his phone on the nightstand.

In the morning, Zeke safely saw the little family to their hotel room and then drove to police headquarters, where he introduced himself to Detective Scott, who would head the case. He filled him in on the facts so far. He also reiterated that he could be an eyewitness once they arrested the bomber.

He headed south on the highway, all he wanted to do was get home to his Margie.

32
A STICKLER FOR PROMPTNESS

Mark and Charlie stopped by the resort office before they went to the cabin. Charlie wanted to pick up some cigarettes. The clerk who rang them up called to them as they left, "Oh by the way, take this and see if any of your group left it here the last time. The judge says it doesn't belong to him. I thought maybe someone else in the group might have left it." Chuck took the ivory-handed knife and showed it to Charlie. "It looks pretty expensive."

Charlie grabbed the knife. "You know, I did see one of the guys with this last time we were here. I'll see that he gets it. Thanks."

"I didn't see anyone with that knife," Mark said as they strolled to the car.

"Neither did I. But since it's lost, I might as well claim it. It's really a nice piece of work." Charlie stuck it in his back pocket.

The men were gathered around the fire waiting for them. Mark immediately apologized when he saw the glower on the judge's face. He knew their host was a stickler for promptness. Judge Kildeer had called for an emergency meeting and the men were unsure what it was about.

Kildeer pounded his gavel on the coffee table. He did not look pleased.

"Let's begin. I think we might have a little problem. It appears some people may have been snooping around the premises. I have their photos in my cell phone. The woman was supposedly in the woods photographing birds the same day we were in the cabin. Then two days later they rented the place for two days. The younger man looked familiar to me, and then it occurred to me that he might have been in my courtroom. Sure enough, I found him in the directory of local attorneys. His name is Jack Manley. He closed down his law practice after his wife died. He now owns a travel agency in Cincinnati. I am going to pass this around. Take a good look. Let me know if you recognize any of them."

The first three men shook their heads "no" and passed it on. Mark did a double take. "What the hell! That's my ex-wife. How the shit is she involved in this?" He began to feel sick to his stomach. The fear of getting caught pressed heavy on him.

The judge pounded the gavel more out of anger than wanting order. His voice came forth hard and cold. "Yes, how did that happen, Mark? Pass along the phone."

Mark did as he was told, remembering his time in jail and how hard it was to get to where he was today. He was beginning to think he shouldn't have trusted the judge. The next two men showed no recognition. When it was passed to Charlie, he stared for a few minutes. "I'm not sure but I think this babe was in the store asking me for help. You don't forget a looker like this one. It's probably a coincidence. Lots of people shop in our store."

There was another slam of the gavel, as the judge's face reddened. "There's no such thing as coincidences, Charlie. Pass it on to Steve."

The last man looked at it and said there was nothing familiar about any of them.

Their leader looked at Max. "You might as well have a look too." Max walked over and grabbed the phone. "Holy shit," Max exclaimed. "The old guy came out of nowhere when I was backing out of Meg's driveway. He looked right at me. That explains why there were no deaths on the news. This guy must have saved them."

The judge slammed down the gavel. "Okay we need to come up with a plan. We need to talk to these people and find out what they know. Max, get them here to the cabin."

Max was already kicking himself in the ass about the bomb. He should have found another way. This was the second bomb that back-fired on him. "I'm on it. How soon do you want them?"

"Right now wouldn't be fast enough." The gavel came down hard.

ANNETTE LACKNER

33
ABDUCTION

Jack had not left Gwen's side since they had found out about the list. He brought her along to his house while he picked up some clothes and checked things out. While he was in the bedroom packing, Gwen started putting perishables into grocery bags. A ski-masked figure in the bushes watched her through the side of the window.

Jack returned to the front of the house and set his suitcase down by the door. "Does this mean we are officially moving in together?" He came over and put his arms around Gwen. "I love you."

The man in the bushes could feel his manhood as he watched Jack put his hands on Gwen's bottom and press her to him.

Gwen smiled and handed him a grocery bag. "Get busy. The sooner we get home the sooner we get to bed."

Max watched them leave and then got in his car and slowly followed them through the neighborhood and on to Gwen's place.

◦ ◦ ◦ ◦ ◦

Ethel was waiting on the counter, meowing for attention. "Why don't you feed her? She's beginning to like to you." Gwen started putting the groceries in the fridge.

"That's because I'm becoming her food source." Jack began to fold up the grocery bags.

"I thought it was your good looks."

"Well, I guess it's that too." He tilted his head and smiled.

Gwen returned the smile and took his hand. "C'mon, handsome, let's get to bed."

"Let me check the locks first. I feel much better since I put a dead-bolt on the door."

They climbed into bed together and made love. Afterward, Gwen turned on some old episodes of *I Love Lucy* and they both fell asleep with Ethel keeping their feet warm.

Outside, the stranger covered himself with a sleeping bag and fell asleep in his car, fantasizing about Gwen.

*   *   *   *   *

Jack woke up early. He glanced over at Gwen who was still in a deep sleep. He couldn't believe how lucky he was to have found her and that from now on he would wake up to see that little blond head poking out from under the down comforter. He tiptoed out of the room and gently closed the door. Jack fumbled through her cabinets, looking for the coffee, and finally had a fresh pot brewing. In a caffeine-deprived fog, he went to the door to grab the morning paper, first looking through the peephole to make sure there was no one outside. He opened the door and as he bent down to pick up the paper, he felt a sharp pain on the back of his head, then everything went blank.

Gwen could smell the coffee as she put on her robe. Ethel ran out when she opened the bedroom door. There was no sign of Jack. "Jack? Where are you? Jack?" Suddenly she felt someone grab her and with one giant motion slap duct tape across her mouth. She tried to fight him off, but she was outmatched. He bent her arm behind her back until she thought it would break.

"Jack is outside taking a little nap. Now, if you want him to wake up from his little nap, put your other hand behind your back so I can tie you up."

Instinctively, she wriggled and kicked, but he pushed her arm farther behind her back. Ethel came running out of nowhere, jumped on the intruder's shoulder and scratched his face. With one fling of his hand Ethel flew across the room. He had both of Gwen's hands now and was binding them together.

He pushed her against the wall and pressed close, dragging his tongue along her neck. Tears poured down her face as he reached his big paw into her robe and fondled her breasts.

"Don't worry, I'm not going to rape you, at least not yet. I understand from your ex that you don't like it rough, so I'll try to be real nice." He grabbed her coat off the coatrack. "As soon as the coast is clear, we're going to join Jack in the van. You'd like that wouldn't you? Maybe the two of you can screw in the back during our ride."

The next thing she knew he was dragging her outside. When he opened the back doors, there was Jack, gagged and tied up. The attacker shoved her in next to Jack and winked. "Have fun back here, kids."

For the next several hours they jostled and banged while trying somehow to reach each other and get loose. When they felt the van going over a gravel road and come to a sudden stop, they knew they had reached their destination. The doors flew open and they were yanked out at gunpoint. They were at the cabin in the woods.

ANNETTE LACKNER

34
A DOG WITH A BONE

Margie was fixing Zeke something to eat while he texted Jack and Gwen again and again. There was no response. He went into his tracking app and was relieved to find they were at Gwen's apartment. He showered, put fresh clothes on and joined Margie for some eggs and waffles. Between bites he related the entire previous day.

"Oh my God, Zeke, you could have been killed by that bomb! Can't you leave this to the police?" Even though she said it, she knew it was useless. Zeke was like a dog with a bone. He wouldn't let it go, not her Zeke.

"They're on it now. We just have to find this creep. I can be an eyewitness. He's toast." The cell phone sitting next to him on the table rang. It was his friend Mike from the station.

"Zeke, I got some matches from the computer on those prints you gave me. One is Charlie Bulleck, arrested for beating his wife. The second match is really interesting. It belongs to Max Chaney. He's ex-CIA. His bio says he was good at disguises and stuff like that. It seems he got into some trouble and was demoted. He quit a few years later and went to work for a private military installation called OCTOPUS. The third match was a little puzzling. It belongs to Judge Robert Paul Kildeer. What kind of shit have you gotten into?"

"It's deep, I'll tell you that. Could you fax photos and prints to Detective Scott at the Michigan State Police as soon as we hang up?"

"Sure. Consider it done."

Zeke immediately went to his laptop and googled OCTOPUS. He scrolled down to the board of directors. Bingo! Kildeer's father was on the list. It was all coming together like a puzzle.

Zeke went to the closet and took down his gun from the top shelf. The old police-issue .38 had been sitting up there for a long time. He loaded it and secured the holster over his shoulder, then put on his coat.

Margie grabbed Zeke's hand. "I don't like the sound of this. Please tell me you're being very careful."

"Not to worry, Margie. Right now, I have to run over to Gwen's apartment and fill them in on what happened in Michigan. Somehow or another we're going to nail this guy."

He gave Margie a kiss and rushed out the back door, leaving her to wring her hands in her apron and start to worry even more as she cleaned up the breakfast dishes. Automatically she said a little prayer from her childhood for his guardian angel to protect him.

35
INQUISITION

Gwen's eyes scanned the room. It was set up like some sort of a meeting, with several men lined up in three rows of chairs. Her heart raced when she saw Mark sitting there with a big grin on his face. She also spotted Charlie, the creep she had been tailing. No one else was familiar except the distinguished man in front of them: Judge Kildeer. She turned her eyes to Jack, who squinted at her as if to say, "We'll be okay." She had a feeling there was someone behind them, it almost felt like an evil presence.

The judge banged down a gavel. "This inquiry shall begin." He looked in Gwen's direction, but he was looking behind her. "Max?" The stranger appeared in front of her and grabbed her head by the hair. With one brutal motion he pulled the tape from her mouth. Jack began to squirm in resistance when he saw the red mark across her face.

"Now, my dear, why were you and your friends snooping around here?" the judge asked. "Don't give me that baloney about being a photographer. I called the magazine. They never heard of you."

"I'm new. Whoever you talked to must not have recognized my name."

The judge stiffened. "Max?"

Max grabbed hold of her neck and slapped her across the face so hard she felt like her jaw was broken.

"Let's try again, Gwen," the judge uttered in a soft, patient voice.

"Honestly! I don't know what you think but…"

"Max."

Another slap that felt even stronger than the one before.

The gavel went down. "Let's try again. We know you're not a photographer. We know your boyfriend Jack is an attorney and we know you've been watching our friend Charlie. What we don't know is why?"

Tears were streaming down, stinging Gwen's raw cheeks. She said nothing.

"I had hoped we wouldn't have to use a less palatable persuasion, my dear, but you leave us no choice. Max, would you bring Jack over to the game table please?"

Gwen watched in horror as Max grabbed Jack and sat him at the table. He then reached into a backpack and pulled out duct tape and a hammer. He untied Jack's hands and placed one of them on the table, unrolled some duct tape and taped his left hand to the table. Jack tried to resist, but his arms were tied to his body. With one mighty blow, Max banged the hammer down on Jack's little finger. Jack writhed in pain, trying not to pass out.

"Stop!" Gwen screamed out. "I'll tell you what you want to know!"

The judge smiled broadly. "I thought that might change your mind. Proceed."

"I knew your wife, Julia, from a support group for abused women. I knew she was very happy about leaving for Maryland and starting her life over. When I saw her death notice in the paper, I couldn't believe it. She had so much to live for. I wouldn't have known she was your wife if her picture hadn't been in the paper. Her sister thought it was suspicious too. She felt you might have had something to do with it. Then when Maura died in Chicago it seemed odd. She, too, had left Cincinnati to start over after attending an abuse support group. I was following Charlie because he threatened his wife, and she went missing. Her mother hired my boss to find her."

The gavel came down with a bang. The judge appeared to be furious.

"Charlie, you broke one of our rules. That will require punishment." Charlie jumped up from his chair, looking for some way to escape the cabin, but he was immediately pushed back down by two of the other men.

"Gwen, who is your boss and how much evidence has he accumulated?" the judge asked.

Gwen was terrified. She couldn't incriminate Zeke and put him in danger. She looked at Jack and hesitated.

"Max."

As Gwen screamed, the hammer came down on the next finger. As Jack writhed in pain, Max looked at her and smiled from ear to ear.

ANNETTE LACKNER

36

NO TIME TO WASTE

He breathed a sigh of relief when he saw Gwen's and Jack's cars parked in front of the apartment complex. He couldn't wait to share his big news. He rang the doorbell and waited. He rang it again, getting uneasy. He rang again and listened for any sound of someone inside. When he started to knock, the door eased open. Someone had left without locking it. Zeke removed his revolver from its holster and slowly, quietly pushed the door open all the way. No signs of a struggle anywhere. He walked soundlessly through the rest of the apartment, fearing what he might discover.

The bed had been slept in but wasn't made. Making his way to the bathroom, he found no sign of damage. Then he noticed Gwen's cell phone on the night table in its holder, charging. He knew she wouldn't go out without her phone. He went through the rooms again. On the kitchen counter he discovered Jack's wallet, cell phone and car keys. This wasn't looking good.

He was startled by a sound: a loud, urgent "MEOW." A limping calico cat emerged from behind the counter. The animal cautiously advanced toward the detective. Zeke picked Ethel up and began to stroke her. "What went on here, pussy cat?"

Ethel meowed again, as if trying to answer.

"I think our friends have been abducted and we need to get you to a vet." Quickly he scanned the magnets on the refrigerator until his eyes located one for a vet. Zeke immediately called Margie, gave her Gwen's address and asked her to pick up the cat and take it to the vet. He promised to call her from the road. He placed Ethel in the bathroom and closed the door. Zeke didn't have any time to waste.

37

MARGIE

Margie was up to her elbows in wrapping paper and gifts. After Zeke left she needed something to keep her busy. *He took his gun*, she thought. *He took his gun.*

She held up a darling pink dress she had bought her granddaughter for Christmas. She smiled, picturing the little girl dancing around the living room in it. She pulled out the wrapping paper adorned with cute little running reindeer. Margie thought about all of the Christmases when she wrapped presents and prayed at the same time, fearing Zeke might not make it home for the holiday. "Stop it," she told herself. "Zeke knows how to take care of himself, he'll be careful. But, the gun, he took his gun." Just as she started to cut through the paper the phone rang. She was relieved to hear her husband's voice.

"Margie, I need you to do something for me. I'm at Gwen's place. It looks like she and Jack have been abducted. I need to get out of here fast. I think I know where I can find them."

"Oh my God, Zeke. Please call for some help. Please!" She wondered what kind of case he had gotten himself into.

"I'm calling for help along the way. I promise. Look, Gwen's cat looks like she's been hurt. She needs to get to a vet. I found a magnet for one on Gwen's refrigerator. See if you can get the cat to them." He rattled off Gwen's address. "The door isn't locked. I closed the cat in the bathroom. I'll call you back from the road later on, okay?"

"Sure, Zeke, sure. I'll leave right away. Be careful. Zeke, I love you."

"Love you right back! Now, go save the damn cat."

His phone went dead.

She had to collect herself. "Calm down, he'll be okay." She freshened herself, grabbed her coat and purse and headed for the garage, then realized she left the address laying on the table. She went back into the house and grabbed it, thinking she had to calm down and get to Gwen's place.

Fortunately, Margie knew her way around the city. She'd lived there all of her life. She recognized the street name. She had taken Debbie to guitar lessons many years ago in this neighborhood. After pulling over several times to check house numbers, she found the apartment complex. *You dodo*, she thought, *why didn't you use your cell phone for directions?*

She parked the car and followed the numbers until she reached Gwen's apartment. She tapped on the door, and just as Zeke said, it slowly opened. Her heart was in her throat even though she knew Zeke would never send her somewhere if he thought it was dangerous.

Quietly, she tiptoed inside and closed the door behind her. She could smell coffee and went into the kitchen. The automatic brewer had started re-heating. She turned it off and rinsed out the pot and placed it in the drainer sitting in the kitchen sink.

Everything looked in order in the living room. "I better call the vet before I get the cat," she thought. She looked on the refrigerator. There was the magnet: Parkway Animal Clinic. Margie dialed the number and explained the situation as best she could without sounding too crazy. She was given directions and told them she was on her way.

"Now, let's hope the cat will come to me."

She opened the bathroom door to a pair of yellow eyes scrutinizing her every move. The cat didn't move. She knelt down on the floor next to the animal and started petting her. She kept her voice soft and reassuring. "It's okay, kitty. It's okay." She continued until she heard a soft purr. "We have to get you to the vet." Gently she picked Ethel up and continued to stroke her fur. Margie spotted a sweater laying across a chair. She picked it up and wrapped it around Ethel thinking the scent of Gwen might be calming. "Oh my God, let Gwen be okay," she prayed.

The vet's office was right down the street. They immediately asked for her ID and had her sign a paper saying she agreed to pay all of the costs, then ran her credit card through their machine to make sure it was valid. Ethel was whisked away and she was told to take a seat. The only one available was between someone with a German shepherd straining on his leash and a young woman holding a cat in its cage. She began silently praying for Zeke and wondering what in the heck she was doing here.

Margie thought of their old dog, Laddie. How they loved that dog. When they had to have her put down, Zeke cried like a baby. He could never bring himself to get another dog. The pain of losing one was more than he could bear.

She glanced at her phone… nothing from Zeke.

Twenty minutes later she was called into Dr. Reinhart's office. She was very young and wholesome looking. Margie was sure she was a vegetarian, a jogger and drank gallons of water every day.

"We think her hip is dislocated, so we are going to keep her for at least a day. We will anesthetize her and try to correct it. Let's hope that takes care of it. If not, we may have to consider surgery. Did you give them your number out front?"

"Yes, but I'll double check on my way out. Thank you, Doctor."

On the drive home, she called Zeke. She couldn't get through. He was probably talking to someone else. She said another prayer for Zeke and Jack and Gwen. "This is what I signed up for when I married a policeman."

ANNETTE LACKNER

38
SENTENCE

"Okay, okay! I'll tell you everything." Gwen was hysterical. "Just call off that beast of yours."

"That's much better, Gwen. I'm listening." The judge leaned back in his chair as if he had all the time in the world.

"I work for Zeke Bailey," she said through tears. "He's a private detective. I'm the one who put it all together; Julia's death, Maura's murder, Meg's disappearance, and then when I discovered Gina's first husband had served time for abuse, I realized that, somehow, they were all connected. I was watching Charlie's apartment when I saw Mark pick him up in hunter's gear. Mark wasn't a hunter. So, I followed them here. I took pictures from outside the window. When I downloaded them, Zeke recognized your friend from hanging out around Meg's house in Michigan, so we rented the cabin to look for clues. We lifted fingerprints and went through the trash. We found a list stuffed inside an empty beer can. Meg's name was the first and my name was the last. Zeke went to Michigan to keep watch over Meg and Jack stayed with me. That's all I know." Gwen looked at each man in the room. She boiled over with rage. "What is this?" she screamed. "You've already ruined our lives, you bastards."

Mark jumped out of his chair. "You bitch! You ruined my life. I couldn't get a job anywhere once I had a record. I could have played football with the pros!"

"You killed our baby." Gwen's crying was out of control. "You killed our baby!"

"I should have killed you too," Mark snarled.

"You almost did!"

The judge pounded the gavel and ordered Mark to sit down.

"*Order!*" the judge demanded. "Gwen, all of the women on the list, including you, have been found guilty by a jury of your peers, guilty of ruining the lives of these men." He continued, as if explaining a sentence in court. "All they wanted was respect. They're very old fashioned. The Bible says women should obey and submit to their husbands. Each one of these men provided well for their wives and in return they wanted a respectable home and meals on the table. For example, I gave my own wife everything she could want, but like the rest of you she was never satisfied. She took me for three million dollars when she left."

"After you beat her to a pulp and locked her up for days! Where is that in the Bible?" Gwen shrieked at Kildeer.

"It's obedience. When someone disobeys there must be punishment. Even though the law favors women, we do not."

Gwen spit directly at his face.

Kildeer removed a hanky from his pocket and slowly wiped it off. "You have already been found guilty. Unfortunately, because you involved your friends in this matter, they will have to be taken care of as well."

The judge looked out at the men. "Are you ready for me to pass a sentence?"

Mark shifted in his chair. He was getting nervous. This wasn't what he had signed up for. Gwen was still alive, so he could back out now and not be an accessory to murder. But after a glance at Max, he realized he was in way over his head. He considered the pain the hitman had inflicted on Jack and came to the conclusion that he had to go along or face deadly consequences.

Ralph's brain was scrambling to find a way out of this. If Maura's death could in some way be traced back to him, he would be in prison for a long, long time. He could kick himself for not leaving this offer on the table. There was no way he would cross the judge or Max at this point. He treasured his life too much.

Despite second thoughts, they all nodded in the affirmative, not knowing what else to do. They certainly couldn't cross their leader, not when he had Max at his side.

"Jack will meet with a little hunting accident here in our lovely forest. Jack, I hereby sentence you to death by firing squad." The gavel slammed down again.

Gwen's thoughts were racing, trying to think of how to save Jack.

"Gwen, you will be the strangler's next victim. You will be raped and strangled by this group of men, at least those who would like to partake. Afterwards your body will be dumped in Eden Park. Another victim of the Cincinnati Strangler."

ANNETTE LACKNER

39
OUR FINEST CLIENTS

He drove the car at breakneck speed. "God, let me get there in time," he prayed under his breath. About an hour away from his destination he called the Michigan State Police.

"Did you get the fingerprint match and photos of our bomber?"

When they answered in the affirmative, he told them where he was going and asked them to notify the nearest police department to be on alert. After he confirmed that the bomber was there, he would call in for an arrest.

He wasn't sure what he was going to be up against. Would it just be the bomber, or would he have others with him, perhaps the judge and some of the men who were there the last time? Whatever, he had to be ready for them.

* * * * *

Michigan State Police Detective Scott was up to his elbows in paperwork and on his fourth cup of black coffee. He had returned to the scene of the bombing at daybreak but didn't come up with anything. His team was scouring the scene for evidence, but Scott realized the suspect was a real pro and there probably wouldn't be any. He had one of his deputies checking out rental agencies in the surrounding area, trying to find out where the white van came from. That would take a while. When he got the call from Zeke Bailey he perked up. He looked again at the prints and the picture of Max Chaney, ex-CIA agent. This case was going to be a big one if what Zeke said was true. The publicity could be quite a feather in his cap. Perhaps it could lead . to a long-awaited promotion.

He phoned his counterpart in Ohio. "This could be a once-in-a-lifetime case. We had a bombing here in Hartsville last night. It turns out there was a Detective Bailey from Cincinnati keeping an eye on a missing girl who had been threatened by her ex. He got her out just in time to save her life. The would-be killer left a Christmas package on the front porch that blew the front door off. Unfortunately, the creep got away."

"Wow, how can we help you here in Ohio?"

"As it turns out, this detective can ID the bomber and he's on his way to locate him as we speak. Zeke thinks he's at a cabin in northern Ohio at a resort called Hunter's Glen. The suspect is an ex-CIA agent with a shadowy record, by the name of Max Chaney. But, even more interesting, Bailey thinks this same guy is involved in a case in Chicago where a woman was beaten and strangled, and also a girl who was strangled while jogging in a Cincinnati park."

"Yeah, I'm familiar with that case. It was right before Thanksgiving. They haven't found anyone yet. You're right this could be a big one."

"There's more. Keep this confidential. He also says that a prominent Cincinnati judge, whose ex-wife died in an accident in Maryland, may be involved and that her death probably wasn't an accident."

"Any proof?" The voice on the other end of the line sounded hesitant.

"Not yet, but Bailey seems to think if he can get Max Chaney it might all prove out."

There was a moment of silence on the other end. "So, this Bailey guy thinks these cases are all connected to the bomber."

"He's almost certain, but here's where we have to be careful. The judge is none other than David Paul Kildeer."

"Oh my God, not the retired senator's son? They own half of Ohio. You're damn right we have to be careful. We have to be one hundred percent absolutely sure or our heads will be on top of one of the Kildeer monuments they have erected all over the state."

Scott lowered his voice. "If we get Chaney, and Bailey is right, it will all shake out. But meanwhile, when Bailey arrives at the cabin, and texts me to confirm that Chaney is there, I'll text you to send backup assistance. It could get ugly. I'm thinking it will be about an hour or so, so be on the ready to send men in."

"I know the exact place you're talking about. Only the very elite own cabins there. I'll put the closest police department on alert stat."

* * * * *

Zeke pulled up and parked at the bottom of the road, making sure he had his phone and his gun. He stayed at the edge of the woods and little by little crept up toward the cabin area, taking note that the same cars that were in the photos were parked in front. Not good news; it meant that they were all here. He waited and got a sense of things, then made a dash for the porch. The drapes were open. He edged along the wall revolver in hand and peeked in as much as he could from the side of the window.

He saw them right away. Gwen was on the sofa. She was wearing only a robe and Zeke could see bruises on her face. It looked like her hands were tied. Jack was tied up and gagged. It looked like his hand was taped to a table. There was a bloody mess around his left hand. His eyes strained, hoping to see Max. He waited patiently and finally he saw him. Zeke took out his phone and rang Scott. "Send them in," he whispered, "our boy is here."

Two men were pulling Jack to his feet. They were dragging Jack toward the front door. Zeke quickly slipped around to the sidewall of the cabin. When they were far away enough to come into his line of sight, Zeke realized one of them was carrying a hunting rifle. It was Max. He ducked down low and ran into the woods. He had to keep them in sight until the police arrived. He didn't want to leave Gwen alone, but he had to help Jack and watch Max.

Gwen remained on the sofa, terrified. Her mind was racing. She tried to remember what the bedroom looked like. Was there anything on the night table that she could use to defend herself? Surely they would have to untie her hands to rape her. "Think, Gwennie, think!"

"Do you want to be first, Mark?" The judge's voice was cool and aloof.

"Nah, I've had this bitch hundreds of times. She's not as special as she thinks she is.

Why don't you go first, Charlie? You think she's such a hot babe."

Charlie jumped up. "You don't have to ask me twice. When I get done with her, she'll be begging for more."

The judge slammed down his gavel. "You're all welcome to a piece of her after Charlie."

He looked down at his watch. "You have exactly two hours, then this whole place gets torched."

Charlie yanked her up off the sofa. As he pulled her down the hall, she noticed something shiny in his back pocket. It was a pocketknife. She would have to get to it without him noticing. She recalled some of the games her second husband liked to play. There had to be some way to get to it. She was desperate, knowing she had to get to Jack somehow before they killed him.

Meanwhile, Zeke followed behind the men as they went farther into the forest. Thank God Jack had on a white T-shirt. It made it easier to keep sight of him. They went deeper into the woods and stopped. They pushed Jack against a tree and tied him to it. Jack didn't look too good. He looked like he was ready to pass out. Zeke rushed in closer so he could get a good shot if he had to. The three men walked back several feet away.

"How does it feel to know you're going to meet your maker, law boy?" Max aimed the rifle directly at Jack's heart, lingering just a second to savor the kill.

Jack started praying. He tightened every muscle in his body to prepare for the bullet. He asked God to save Gwen, please save Gwen. He could see the barrel of the gun aiming, ready to shoot. He closed his eyes, trying to conjure up Gwen's face.

Jack heard the discharge, but felt nothing. Was he dead? Was it over that fast? He opened his eyes to see Max doubled over in pain. The other men scattered. Zeke came out of nowhere and held his pistol against Max's head. "Don't reach for that rifle or I'll blow your head off!" There was blood pouring from Max's shoulder. Zeke kicked the weapon out of Max's reach. He grabbed Max by the belt and dragged the bleeding man over to Jack. "Now pull the tape off his mouth." Max took the bloody hand that had been holding his wounded shoulder and ripped off the tape.

Zeke kept his gun on Max's temple. "I'm sorry but I need to put you out of commission. Step back a foot." The hitman obeyed, keeping his eyes on the gun. Zeke kicked him in the groin with all the force he could muster. As Max howled, bending over in agony, Zeke fought a strong urge to inflict more pain by shooting him in the knee. Instead, the enraged detective banged him over the head with his pistol.

"Good job," murmured Jack, as Zeke untied him. "You should have killed the bastard."

"I'd rather see him fry."

Jack looked very pale. "What about the other guys?"

"I'm sure they're long gone. They won't want any part of what's coming down. What are we up against in the house?"

Jack started to reel. He sat down on the forest floor. "The judge and his lemmings planned this whole thing. They were going to kill me. We've got to get to Gwen. They're going to rape and strangle her. Oh God, we might be too late." Jack tried to get up, but Zeke gently pushed him down against the tree.

"I have police backup coming. You stay here with the rifle and keep an eye on this scumbag." Zeke gave Max a kick in the ribs to make sure he was still out cold. "I've got to try to get into the cabin somehow."

* * * * *

Charlie pushed Gwen through the door, closed it and locked it. He yanked her robe down to her waist. "Pretty nice," he panted as he took in her bare torso.

"Charlie, honey, you think you can make me beg for more?" She sweetened her voice. "Maybe I can make you beg for more. Let's not rush this. We've got two hours if we want. There's more than one way to screw, you know." She stared down at his crotch. "Untie my hands, Charlie," she commanded in a throaty, sexy voice.

"Oh, babe, you are something." He did what she asked, contemplating her hands following the direction of her eyes.

"I have to keep stalling," Gwen thought. "Let's take this real slow. Take off your shoes, Charlie…" He stepped out of his loafers. Gwen began undressing him. She laid his jeans on the edge of the bed and sat him down next to them. Then she straddled him, eyeing the pocketknife, making sure she could reach it. Her skin crawled as he started kissing her breasts. *Keep him occupied. I have to get to Jack.* Charlie started biting. She groped for the weapon and put her arms around his neck. "Oh, Charlie, you really know how to please a girl."

With both hands around his neck, she was able to open the knife. He started to push her up and down against him. As she raised the knife, there was a wailing of sirens in the distance. *Do it now!* She thrust the ivory-handled blade between his shoulder blades. He screamed as she jumped away from him. Charlie lurched at her but was in too much pain to make contact. Gwen ran for her robe, shaking and sobbing.

Charlie was still trying to get off the bed as she bolted through the door.

* * * * *

Still charged with a rush of adrenalin, Zeke ran through the woods back to the cabin. He wasn't sure what to do, Gwen's life might hang in the balance. He drew his gun from the holster and crept up to the door. The element of surprise was all he had. As he reached for the handle, he could hear the sirens of the approaching police back-up. He shoved open the door and pointed his gun directly at the judge.

"Hands in the air, NOW!"

The judge looked up in disbelief, raising his hands as commanded. "Look, I don't know what you think is going on, but...."

The remaining men sat frozen in their seats. The sirens were just outside the door.

"Just shut up. Where is Gwen?"

The judge hesitated.

"Where is she?" yelled Zeke.

Gwen stumbled into the room just as the arriving police started handcuffing and reading rights to the fake jurors. "I'm right here. Where's Jack, Zeke? Where's Jack?" She collapsed into Zeke's arms.

"He's okay. He's in the woods holding a gun on the killer. I'll take an officer with me and bring him back. You sit down and take it easy. Okay?"

He left the cabin, escorted by two of the policemen.

Gwen sat down on the nearest chair, still in a daze. "You need to go into the bedroom. I just stabbed someone." She dropped her head into her trembling hands and began to sob.

The judge was in the state of denial. "Do you know who I am? I can have you fired for this. I have friends in high places who will help me, damn it! This is all a big mistake."

"You can call your lawyer when we get to headquarters." The man in blue didn't seem too interested in what the judge had to say.

Gwen saw Zeke walking toward the porch with Jack leaning on him. She ran out to the porch to greet them, laughing and sobbing at the same time. "Oh, thank God," she cried over and over. She took Jack in her arms and held him. Then she sat him down on one of the wicker chairs.

Several minutes later, an ambulance and several more police cars arrived at the scene. Officers immediately scattered into the woods to round up the men who had fled. Zeke instructed the EMT's to take a stretcher to pick up Max. Gwen and Jack watched as Zeke helped load the handcuffed judge and the "jury of his peers" into the police vehicles. Unlike his fake jury, who took the words "you have the right to remain silent" seriously, the judge was still carrying on and on. "This is outrageous! I am a *judge*. My father is a *senator*. You don't know who you're messing with." Zeke slammed the cruiser door to his rants and returned to the porch.

"He's not too happy, is he?" He sat down next to his friends.

"You think he's upset now, just wait until Gwen and I file a civil suit against him." Jack's face turned beet red. "We are going to take that bastard for everything he's got!"

"Calm down, Jack." Gwen began to give his shoulder gentle pats. "Right now, we just need to get you taken care of."

"We're going to need another ambulance," Zeke observed as medics came out of the woods carrying a stretcher. Max was still out cold. They loaded him beside Charlie and started to administer what first aid they could. Zeke smiled at Jack. "Can you hold on until the next one gets here? I don't think you care to ride in the same one as these scumbags."

"You've got that right. Take them away." He waved his towel-wrapped hand at the ambulance drivers. The lights flashed and the siren wailed as they drove down the gravel road.

Zeke brought them a drink of water and sat down beside his friends. "Sorry it isn't something stronger. I'll follow the two of you to the hospital and then check in with the local police. I'll need to fill in the report and also claim a missing possession."

Jack looked up at Zeke. "What missing possession?" He was beginning to get his color back.

Zeke laughed out loud. "Who would have thought I would find it in the back of Gwen's assailant! My ivory-handled pocketknife. Unfortunately, it's now police evidence."

Gwen started trembling all over again. She couldn't believe she had actually stabbed someone. Then she began to laugh and cry at the same time.

Chuck, the office manager, looked up from his crossword puzzle when he heard a gunshot in the woods thinking that the judge and his friends were out hunting. But when he heard sirens and saw several police cars speed past the office, he left his post, not bothering to lock up, and followed them to the cabin. He watched from the safety of his vehicle as the police charged the cabin and made their arrests. When it was all over and he saw Zeke bring Jack to the porch, he got out and walked over to them. "What the heck happened here? The judge and his friends are some of our finest clients. An event like this could take the whole property's value down."

Zeke approached him getting right in his face. "You'll read about it in the papers tomorrow." The second ambulance approached before Chuck could say more. The EMTs went immediately to Jack to check him out before they took him to the waiting transport. Gwen climbed in and sat next to Jack, while Zeke got in his car and called Margie. "I'm okay, honey. I'm okay." God, he hated to hear Margie cry. "I'll call you back later, when I know what time I'll be home. I love you."

Chuck was still standing outside of his car, his face was beet red. All he could think about was the bad publicity this incident would bring. He could lose his job over this. "If there's any damage inside, someone's going to have pay for it," he yelled at Zeke's car as it passed.

Zeke leaned out his window and yelled, "Tell it to the judge." He followed the wailing ambulance down the gravel road.

40
THE GALAPAGOS ISLANDS

They looked like ordinary newlyweds, except for the bandages and metal splints jutting out from the husband's left hand. They leaned on the ship's rail, looking out at the tranquil turquoise sea.

"Beautiful," sighed Gwen. "You know, when I first met you, I wondered what it would be like to go to exotic places with you." They had been traveling in Peru and Ecuador for the past three weeks. Jack took Gwen to all of the exotic places he had told her about. They climbed Machu Pichu together, boated on Lake Titicaca, shopped in Otavalo and spent time touring Ecuador's capital city, Quito, before starting their voyage to the Galapagos Islands.

He smiled, "And I wondered what it would be like to have you share exotic places with me."

They both reached for a glass of fresh watermelon juice, one of the local specialties, offered to them by one of the ship's waiters.

"The wedding was beautiful, wasn't it?" Gwen took a sip of the refreshing drink. It was a quiet wedding with Jack's son and his girlfriend Tracy, Ali and her intended, and Zeke and Margie in attendance.

"I can't think of a better way to celebrate New Year's Eve."

Jack's cell phone rang. He could see it was Zeke. His good thumb hit the answer button. He pressed speaker and put the phone between their ears.

"Hi, Zeke. What's up?"

"Good news. Max cut a deal. He squealed like the rat that he is. Rather than get the death penalty he will testify about the whole thing for the county prosecutor. He named them all and explained how it came down. The judge and his friends are going away for a long, long time. It's all over the news outlets. Everyone in town is talking about it, and as far as I'm concerned it couldn't have happened to a nicer guy."

"Zeke, that's great news!" Gwen was overjoyed.

"And I'll never buck a woman's intuition again, Gwen."

She laughed. "I am going to hold you to that."

"Well, I better let you two lovebirds get back to your honeymoon. Besides, Margie and I have to start packing for Bermuda. She's as excited as a teenager. Talk to you when we are all back in town."

"That's a deal." Jack disconnected the call.

A second later a text came through. They looked down to see Ethel staring at them with her wide yellow eyes. The caption read: "Vet checked her out today. She's 100 percent AOK."

The two smiled and looked back out to the sea. A school of dolphins was flipping in and out of the calm waters. They watched in wonder, and Gwen rested her head on Jack's shoulder.

"It doesn't get any better than this!"

ACKNOWLEDGEMENTS

I am keenly aware that this book wouldn't have come to fruition without the help of others.

My sincere thanks to my family for their continuing support in this project, particularly my daughter Laura Saylor, granddaughter Andi Saylor and grandson Hank Saylor for their "tech support." I'd also like to thank those who volunteered to read the many re-writes, namely, Nanci Davis and my son-in-law Philip Laird. Their suggestions and encouragement kept me moving forward.

Also, much appreciation to Amy Peters Thomas, who advised me on the legal aspects of the book, and Bill O'Brien for his legal advice.

Last, but not least, my fellow writers at Women Writing for (a) Change here in Cincinnati. They listened to this story from beginning to end, helping me craft it into a finished product. A special shout-out to Dee Garretson, who read it, suggested changes to make it a better manuscript, and spent much of her valuable time talking me through the publishing process.

ANNETTE LACKNER

BOOK CLUB DISCUSSION QUESTIONS

1. Do you know anyone who has suffered abuse by their spouse? Discuss.

2. Do you feel the "Me, Too" movement has given women a voice on these issues? How do you think it has affected men?

3. The author paints a disturbing picture of several men in this book. Do you feel she redeems herself with her portrayal of Jack and Zeke?

4. Zeke is pretty "old school." Do you think he is a good representation of older men?

5. Do you think men like Max are inherently evil, or do you think evil develops in a person through their life experiences?

6. Gwen distrusts Jack at first. As a reader, did you feel the same way about him?

7. Gwen blames herself for her first two marriages. Is there any truth to these feelings?

8. The judge forms a plot to get revenge on his wife. Do you think he could have executed the plan without power and money?

9. How difficult do you think it would be for a woman to get out of an abusive situation?

10. How difficult do you think it would be to marry again after a woman has experienced such abuse in a former marriage?

11. Jack falls in love with Gwen because, despite her vulnerabilities, she garnered the strength to go on with her life. Do you agree with his assessment?

12. Money and power are used for evil by the judge and Gwen's second husband in this book. Talk about ways that money and power can be used for good.

13. In the beginning of the story, Gwen feels that Jack is almost too good to be true. Did you ever have that feeling about something or someone in your life? How did it turn out?

ABOUT THE AUTHOR

Annette "Toni" Lackner was born and raised in Cincinnati, Ohio where she lives with her husband, Bud. She always enjoyed writing, but didn't get serious about it until she retired from the business world. She attended fiction writing classes at the University of Cincinnati Evening Communiversity and has been a 15-year member of Women Writing for (a) Change, where she continues to hone her writing skills. She is the author of *Edward's Bell*, a short story that won second place in a *Writer's Journal* fiction contest, and *Mrs. Silvernagel's Christmas. A Perfect Day for a Slush*, her one-act play, was performed at Women Writing for (a) Change. Her poetry has appeared in the anthology *For a Better World* over the years. She loves travel and volunteer work and is a member of two book clubs. Her three married daughters have blessed her with six grandchildren who are a constant source of joy.

Made in the USA
Monee, IL
23 May 2022

96904557R00114